DANCING

Caryl Phillips was born ~~~~~~~~~~ now lives in London and New York. *Crossing the River* was shortlisted for the Booker Prize and his most recent novel, *A Distant Shore*, won the 2004 Commonwealth Writers Prize.

www.carylphillips.com

CARYL PHILLIPS

Dancing in the Dark

VINTAGE BOOKS
London

Published by Vintage 2006

10

Copyright © Caryl Phillips 2005

First published in Great Britain in 2005 by
Secker & Warburg

Vintage
Random House, 20 Vauxhall Bridge Road,
London SW1V 2SA

Random House Australia (Pty) Limited
20 Alfred Street, Milsons Point, Sydney,
New South Wales 2061, Australia

Random House New Zealand Limited
18 Poland Road, Glenfield, Auckland 10, New Zealand

Random House (Pty) Limited
Isle of Houghton, Corner of Boundary Road & Carse O'Gowrie,
Houghton, 2198, South Africa

Random House Publishers India Private Limited
301 World Trade Tower, Hotel Intercontinental Grand Complex,
Barakhamba Lane, New Delhi 110 001, India

The Random House Group Limited Reg. No. 954009
www.randomhouse.co.uk/vintage

A CIP catalogue record for this book
is available from the British Library

ISBN 9780099488873 (from Jan 2007)
ISBN 0099488876

Penguin Random House is committed to a sustainable future for
our business, our readers and our planet. This book is made from
Forest Stewardship Council® certified paper.

Printed and bound in Great Britain by Clays Ltd, Elcograf S.p.A.

Nobody in America knows my real name and,
if I can prevent it, nobody ever will.

—BERT WILLIAMS

ACKNOWLEDGMENTS

I wish to acknowledge the help of the Dorothy and Lewis B. Cullman Center for Scholars and Writers at the New York Public Library, which awarded me a Mel and Louis Tukman Fellowship. This enabled me to complete my research for this novel. I have also been dependent upon outstanding work by numerous scholars, in many fields, which has fed my imaginative reconstruction of both individuals and place. However, my biggest debt of gratitude is to Vanessa Garcia, whose helpful suggestions, and thorough research, I grew to value and depend upon.

Prologue

If you walk down Seventh Avenue today he is a man who never existed. On this broad Harlem avenue a torn curtain might stir in response to the tug of a hand. Dark hand, now waving. If you walk down this broad Harlem avenue today it will soon become clear that old-fashioned dignity and civic pride have long fled the scene, and this would have broken his stout heart. Back then he dressed well, he walked tall, and the bright glare from his shoes could pick a man's eyes clean out of his knobby head. Women watched him pass by, his hardback carriage upright, and they whispered half sentences about him from behind perfumed handkerchiefs that they held close to their full lips. But they never eyeballed him, for this was a man who lived way beyond their hips, and it didn't make no sense to look too interested in such a man. Men watched him too, with their collars turned high, pulling on ash-heavy cigarettes, their broad feet helplessly anchored to the earth, but this was a man who looked neither left nor right as he strode through the streets. Children followed him at a respectable distance—down as far as the park—and then their young spirits were seized by the grass, and the trees, and the Harlem reservoir, but the neighborhood *man* continued on his way, stepping purposefully toward his daily rendezvous with midtown business. White man's business. Today, if you walk down this broad Harlem avenue as far as the park, and then continue walking through the park to midtown, he is a man who never existed. He has gone. Back uptown, in his Harlem, a needle-borne pestilence has been visited upon the people. The handsome brownstones have now faded, the streets are unswept, the stores are boarded up, and clumps of weeds search out dull sunlight through broad cracks in the sidewalk. Old-fashioned dignity and civic pride have fled the scene, and this would have broken his stout heart.

In *his* time these wide uptown boulevards, with their agreeably appointed row houses, exuded the quiet civility of an emerging middle-class elegance. The occasional corner boasted a "clean" theater or a bar, but nothing that might alarm the local pastor or disturb the churchgoing population. In *his* time there were no moonlit migrations from downtown, there were no neon signs to bedazzle, no heavily perspiring tuxedoed Negro musicians, and no white men or white women dolled up in fine furs and bright jewels lingering after hours in the hope of an authentic thrill. In *his* time this was a respectable colored world peopled by those who had yet to learn how to grin and bend over for the white man. In this new colored world above the park, this tall, light-skinned man was king, and his subjects were happy to bask in his long ambling shadow.

Proud new twentieth-century world where the four El lines stretched their arms and came right uptown, stitching the great New World city to the suddenly Negro suburb. The Italian baker

and the German brewer and the Irish policeman had no inclina-
tion to travel to, or live in, such a far-flung place, and so some
forty years after the end of the war that was fought to liberate
blistered wrists and ankles, New York City Negroes were finally
becoming American citizens with homes of their own. Peering
through DuBois's newly embroidered veil, they saw before them a
new century and new possibilities above 110th Street, where a
powerful Harlem harmattan was blowing fresh news from Africa.
Tan maidens, with peachy bleached skin and recently straightened hair, stepped around tall muscular men fresh off the ships
from the Caribbean, who in turn rubbed shoulders with excited
southerners who had tilled enough soil for a dozen lifetimes and
were overjoyed to have finally arrived in the north. And then, of
course, there were the formerly enslaved New Yorkers who could
trace their ties with the city back to the entrepreneurial, but
mean-spirited, Dutch. Quick everybody, hurry uptown to the
barbershops and restaurants and funeral homes that colored men
now owned in New York City. Hurry home to Harlem. West
Indian Bert Williams's Harlem. And then, after Bert Williams
left, everything changed and Harlem began to sell her smile, and
her vitality, and her energy, and automobiles began to clubfoot
their way uptown and sit right on down—sometimes they didn't
even have the good sense to turn off their engines—but by then
Harlem was better known to the world as a neighborhood that
one should visit only under the moon, a place where one might
buy a front row seat and witness the clumsy metal hooves of
Bojangles stomping poor Africa to death and replacing her with
Showtime.

And so his world became a famous nighttime venue for people
who wished to purchase a thrill and temporarily escape the cage
in which they lived their ordered downtown lives. They would

climb into their vehicles and ask to be driven uptown in order that they might go back to the jungle and behold tall and terrific women shaking their hips and dancing with an abandon that was beyond the control of a rational mind. They wished to go back to a place that they imagined they had long ago fled on two legs with a silk scarf tossed casually around their necks. The dark past in their city, coons tight like spoons on brightly lit stages, and champagne flowing like the Hudson at full tide. These were bright new monied times in which society people were encouraged to enjoy the primitive theatrics of those who appeared to be finally understanding that their principal role was now to entertain. Listen. The wail of a trumpet as it screeches crazily toward heaven and then shudders and breaks and falls back to earth, where its lament is replaced by the anxious syncopated tap tap tapping of clumsily shod feet beating out their joyous black misery in a tattoo of sweating servitude. Performative bondage. Yes sir, boss, I will be what you want me to be, and when you climb into your automobile at five o'clock in the morning with Miss Ann on your arm, and a gentle buzzing in your veins, the lights will be turned off, and the shoes will be eased from my burning feet, and the spit shaken out of my instrument, and the tie loosened from my fat neck, and we men will appear where previously only shades lived, and we men will speak to one another in grave low tones, cutting fatigue with relief and anticipating short bouts of loving before the chain of streetlights blink out one after the other and the sun clears the horizon and sleep finally reaches down and smoothes our furrowed American brows, bringing us some kind of peace until the afternoon is new and strong and full again.

Act One

(1873–1903)

It is February 1903 and at present he is impersonating Shylock Homestead in the musical *In Dahomey,* but only after dark. He shambles about as though unsure what to do next, as if a wrong turning has placed him upon this stage and he may as well stay put until somebody offers him the opportunity to withdraw. Every evening Mr. Williams wanders aimlessly, but despite his size there is some elegance to his movement. When the audience raises its collective voice and asks him to reprise a song, Mr. Williams acts as though he is first shocked and then somewhat embarrassed that they should be stirring him out of his befuddled anonymity. Of course, this is all the more comical to his audience for they have never before witnessed a Negro performer affecting such indifference in the face of such overwhelming approval. Back uptown in Harlem, few residents have actually seen him perform, but everybody is fully aware of his stellar reputation. However, there are some Harlemites who have sat upstairs in the balcony and looked down at the senior partner in the Williams and Walker comedy duo, who are unsure what to make of his foolish blackface antics. These days Mr. Williams seldom looks up at the parcel of dark faces that stare down at him from nigger heaven, but he is always grateful to hear a good number of these colored Americans applauding enthusiastically as *In Dahomey* unfolds.

He stares at the contented white faces in the orchestra stalls knowing that he can hold an audience like nobody else in the city. He knows when to go gently with them, and he carefully observes their mood; he knows not to strain the color line for he respects their violence. At other times, when he can sense something close to warmth, he might push and cajole a little, and try to show them something that they had not thought of before; he might try to introduce them to the notion that music and wit are the colored man's gift to America, and then impress them with his own unique style of carefree dancing. All the while he listens closely for a single dull note, and should he detect it he will proceed with caution and neither irritate nor provoke. He is keen that at the end of the evening, they should all leave safely and without either party having broken the unwritten contract that exists between the Negro performer and his white audience. If they can achieve this, then it will be possible for them to come together again in good faith. He cares what they think about him, and he understands that one false step and he risks toppling over into the musician's pit and being replaced by Bob Cole or Ernest Hogan or one of the scores of other colored performers who are keen to usurp him without fully understanding that they *do* have the choice of offering these white faces in the orchestra stalls some artistic drollery and a little repose instead of clownish roughness and loud vulgarity.

But these days an increasingly impatient George does not share his partner's circumspect feelings with regard to their white audience. Before *In Dahomey*, neither Williams nor Walker objected to being presented as "The Two Real Coons" on the New York stage. They were young men, freshly arrived in the city and making their determined way in the world of vaudeville, often sharing the boards with acts billed as "The Merry Wops" or "The Sport and the Jew," and when money was in short supply they were happy to play on the same bill with trained dog and monkey acts. But it is now 1903, and times have changed and they are successful, and although Bert does not like to heat up the white man's blood by being flash in his face, George feels differently. George takes the role of the dude of the pair, the Broadway swell with silk cravat and fancy spats who blazes with energy, and who is not afraid to bad eye the audience. He is always pushing and demanding more, and the more George agitates, the more sorrowful his partner becomes both in performance and in person. He thinks, No need to be like that, George, as his gold-toothed partner grins and winks and seems determined to create a palpable flutter of feminine hearts both onstage and in the orchestra stalls, but Bert never says anything to dandy George in his colorful vests. Some days, Bert feels that their act, although seamless and coherent on the outside, is beginning to fracture internally for George has absolutely no interest in going gently with an audience and learning how to seduce them, and Lord help the man, white or colored, who would dare refer to him with an unpleasant epithet. In fact, an increasingly successful, and confident, George is beginning to act as though he doesn't give a damn about white folks.

WALKER: I tell you I'm letting you in on this because you're a friend of mine. I could do this alone and let no one in on it. But I want you to share it just because we're

good friends. Now after you get into the bank, you
fill the satchel with money.

WILLIAMS: Whose money?

WALKER: That ain't the point. We don't know who put the
money there, and we don't know why they got it.
And they won't know how we got it. All you have to
do is fill the satchel; I'll get the satchel—you won't
have nothing to bother about—that's 'cause you're a
friend of mine, see?

WILLIAMS: And what do I do with the satchel?

WALKER: All you got to do is bring it to me at a place where I
tell you.

WILLIAMS: When they come to count up the cash and find it
short, then what?

WALKER: By that time we'll be far, far away—where the birds
are singing sweetly and the flowers are in bloom.

WILLIAMS: *(With doleful reflection)* And if they catch us they'll
put us so far, far away we never hear no birds singin'.
And everybody knows you can't smell no flowers
through a stone wall.

He listens to the applause for his slow and cautious character. He
listens to the applause for George's dapper, city-slick Negro dude.
Do the audience understand that his character, this Shylock
Homestead whose dull-witted antics amuse them, bears no relationship to the real Egbert Austin Williams? Every evening this
question worries him, and every evening as he takes his curtain
call he tries to ignore it, but he often lies in his bed late into the
night trying to calculate where he might force a little more laughter here, or squeeze an inch more room to work with there, and
therefore impress them with the overwhelming evidence of his
artistry. Every evening he listens to the rainstorm of their ap-

plause and every evening he takes his bow, careful to make sure that he bends from the waist in tight unison with George, careful to make sure that the pair of them move and offer their best smile as one. George talks without moving his lips or turning his head. "You want to give them more?" Bert looks straight ahead. "Not tonight." Again they bow as one. "Everything okay?" "Sure, everything is just capital." The band begins to play their number and Bert waves a slow-branched hand to the audience and turns to leave. He holds the curtain open for George and makes sure that his partner passes safely through the velvet drapes. The thunderous applause continues, but Bert does not turn again to look at the audience for, at this moment, he wants something from them that he suspects he can never have: their respect. However, from the very beginning, this reluctant seven-legged word has failed to make an appointment with him.

—Mr. Williams?
He listens to the stage manager hollering out his name in the busy corridor. Why can't the impatient man wait until he has taken off his face?
—Mr. Williams, you'll be wanting me to keep a seat at tomorrow night's performance for your pop?
Every night the same intrusive question, and every night the same polite answer.
—Sure, Mr. Kelly, you keep that seat nice and warm. I reckon he'll be coming back either tomorrow night or some night soon.
He places the newly soiled towel by the bowl of murky water and he stares into the mirror at his fresh, clean face. He knows that his father has no desire to return and witness his son transforming himself into a nigger fool. He knows his father well enough to understand that beneath his placid exterior a quiet frustration burns within him, and he believes that his father does not like to

place himself in situations that might cause him to get heated up. Father and son have never spoken of this fact, but since their arrival in America father and son seem to have found it difficult to communicate on any subject.

—Mr. Williams, will you be needing anything else tonight?

—I don't believe so, Mr. Kelly.

—Well, you just remember. I'll be holding that spot for your pop. Tomorrow night, or whenever he's ready to see you perform, you just let me know.

—Thank you, Mr. Kelly. I surely appreciate it.

He averts his eyes from the mirror and listens to the sound of retreating footsteps in the corridor beyond his locked dressing room door. Although no words have been exchanged between them, it is clear that his bewildered father is deeply ashamed of his only son.

The balance has gone. Five years ago, when she first met him, young Mr. Williams was a man with a purpose. Handsome, well dressed, and still in his mid-twenties, he possessed courtesies that belonged to an earlier era. He rose early, and retired early, and drank and smoked only in moderation, and he possessed a fierce ambition and work ethic. And talent. Lord, he had a talent that others could see, but none, she believed, could imagine it in full bloom the way she could. This, she thought, was a man fit for a widow who had already mastered the art of nurturing a man's dreams. This new man had traveled a long way from his Caribbean birthplace and twice crossed America, first to the west and then back to the east. This was a man whose brow she might soothe, a man she could encourage to relax and stay focused as he journeyed toward his destiny. Truly, fate had blessed her, but five years later the balance has gone. On that momentous day she accompanied her friend Ada, and sat quietly in the corner of the photographer's studio. The tobacco advertisement was to feature Ada and another woman, all dressed up in their finery, sophisticated ladies ready to step out on the arms of two gentlemen. Quality colored ladies, quality product, and then the two dandies entered the studio, one tall and tan, one dark and short, and her eyes were drawn to the tall man, who bowed gently before Ada and the other woman and then turned to her and smiled with a sweetness that caused her body to tremble, so much so that Ada had to shoot her foolish friend an unambiguous glare. She lowered her eyes, for there was now no longer any need to look at this tall man for his image was burned deeply into her soul. She had immediately noticed that this lofty man, with long fingers to match his legs, possessed a strange spring in his step. She expected a less nimble gait from a man with his build, something that might betray the fact that he was overly conscious of his size, but there was a curious buoyancy to his movement. She looked up as the photographer set the first pose, and she observed that it was *his* arm that Ada's companion was instructed to take but the woman began to act uppity with him, and then plain downright cold, for she had noticed him looking across at Lottie, but it made no difference for he kept right on treating this difficult woman like a queen upon whom he was honored to attend. Lottie observed that the darker man also had manners, although he did not possess the same courtesies as his taller friend. She scrutinized the darker man and immediately sensed that beneath the sugar he would probably be quick to anger and express his mannishness, and should a woman attempt to slip a noose around his ankle he would soon be stepping clear. A heartbreaker, she thought, but if Ada wished to make reckless eyes at this man, then who was she to say anything? Her friend's new preoccupation left her free to secretly pursue her own interest, although, of course, she had no intention of letting this man know that her heart was already beating to his tune. And yet again the photographer moved this tall man and Ada's tiresome friend into another position that suggested both courtliness and intimacy, and the tall man turned his head so that his eyes once more met those of Lottie, who remained seated quietly in the corner. She reminded herself that whatever thoughts might be coursing through her mind she was a widow and she should not forget herself and allow her heart to fist up so rapidly for this young man.

Sitting across the table from him at a fine restaurant on Fifty-third Street, Lottie melts. But he does not blow any hot air on her. He just listens to what she has to say about her late husband's painful final days in Chicago, and he drinks up her words as though they were the finest red wine. She is helpless in the face of his stillness. He is balanced, and he seems to understand that the first duty of love is to listen. She looks closely at his hands, for she knows that gentle hands that are afraid of loss are the only hands for her. Lottie wishes to apologize for her somewhat coy behavior at the photographer's studio, but saying sorry seems unnecessary. She toys with her food while, inside of her, certainty falls like an anchor.

He insists on walking her the four blocks back to her rooming house on Forty-ninth Street, and as they step out of the restaurant he offers her his arm. They ignore the unsavory odors that emanate hereabouts from dark hallways and open windows, and they promenade regally as though crossing a meadow that is high with the scent of flowers on a bright spring morning. He tells her that there is no other girl; that there has never been another girl, that his life has been selfishly dedicated to performing, but now he is ready for something else. He confesses that her quiet dignity has captured his heart and he wonders if she might consider hitching her fortune to his. She smiles coyly and suddenly he feels overwhelmed with embarrassment. As they reach the junction at Fifty-first Street and Broadway they both hear the word "niggers" fly from a horse-drawn carriage, but neither looks up to investigate what foul mouth has unleashed this missile. The word ricochets off a wall and crosses in front of them, creating a low obstacle over which they both step. They do so without breaking stride and press on toward Lottie's place of residence. Were they to turn around they would still see the word hurtling around the junction of Fifty-first Street and Broadway, picking up speed here, losing tempo there, as purposefully silent as a bird's flight, yet furiously burning energy deep into the New York night.

Before she retires Lottie lights a solitary candle and then kneels by the side of her bed. As the scarf of smoke eddies its way toward the ceiling in swirling fits and starts, she begins to recite her cherished list of names. Her dry lips peel stubbornly apart, and as she whispers the names her now freshly moistened lips brush gently, one against the other. She squeezes her hands together and adds one more name. But what to call him? Mr. Williams? Perhaps she should have given him the opportunity of naming himself, but she knows that Mr. Williams is not this type of a man. "Call me the Honey Man." "They call me Sweet Loving." "Let me be your daddy." For most of her years on the stage she has heard this kind of sweet talk, and a ring, bold and visible on her left hand, has never stopped a man's tongue from flapping. "Baby, they call me the Candy Man." But this man, whose head fame has not yet managed to turn, seems to have no desire to rename himself. She continues to kneel by the side of her bed.

Sitting high up in the balcony with the colored folks, she watches tall, twenty-six-year-old Mr. Williams perform with his partner.

Two Real Coons whooping it up on the New York stage, and a shiver of pride runs through her body. Women of all shades, from nearly night to nearly day, are captivated by the sight of Mr. Walker all prettified in his spats and his vest and his trim jacket, and each evening these ladies return in order to enjoy the thrill of being under the same roof as Jim Dandy. Lottie looks at these women and understands that while they respect the taller man, he can never generate the same heat in their hearts, which pleases Lottie for she knows that some women possess appetites that are dangerous to men. Again Lottie looks at Mr. Williams. Hers is a private passion, studying how he moves, how a raised eyebrow here and a turn of the wrist there make the white folks downstairs collapse into heaps of laughter. They laugh at him, and they feel sorry for him, but *she* understands that they are laughing at somebody else. This is not the dignified man that she knows, and so she too is permitted to laugh. However, the sight of her suitor in corkface disturbs something in her soul. But there is nobody to whom she might turn and quietly confess her anxieties, sitting high up in the balcony with the colored folks.

While his darker partner drank and smoked late into the night, and decided which of his female entourage he should entertain, Bert would have long ago proffered his excuses and climbed the stairs and made his deliberate way up to his single bed at the back of Marshall's Hotel on Fifty-third Street between Sixth and Seventh Avenues. Once there he would first draw the drapes and then slowly contemplate undressing. Each article of clothing was neatly folded and hung on a wooden hanger, and then his long extravagant shoes were carefully lined up, one next to the other. Only then would Bert slide into the white rectangular pocket and prop himself up and read from his extensive book collection. Much to his father's chagrin, Leland Stanford's institution was

already a past dream, but Bert refused to abandon the quest for
self-improvement. Philosophy, history, science, he read books on
whatever subjects took his interest, but eventually the tension of
the day would take its toll, and Bert would prudently mark his
place and then rest his book back on the bedside table. For a few
moments he would lie with his eyes open, staring at the ceiling,
dreaming of songs yet to be written, keen to improve his mime
skills and hone his voice, eager to be recognized. The whole world
lay before him and Lady Luck had dealt him a fine hand for he
truly believed that he was in the right city at the right time. He
believed that if both he and George stepped cautiously, and kept
moving forward, then the theater might well be kind to them, but
of late he worried about George for he appeared to be growing
increasingly impatient. In all the time that they had lived and
worked together as brothers, he had never once seen George back
down in an argument or turn from a fight, and now, as their fame
as the Two Real Coons was beginning to quicken, George seemed
to be reveling in the attention. Bert knew that his partner would
be downstairs in Marshall's Lounge drinking with Bob Cole,
whose performances as "Nigger Bob with chitlin'-loving eyes"
marked him out as one of the crude minstrels whom George pro-
fessed to despise. However, offstage they remained firm friends,
and the pair of them often stayed in Marshall's Lounge until
dawn, leaving only to scamper upstairs and swiftly entertain one
of the many devotees who the pair of them traded like used banknotes. The talk that reached Bert's ears was not good, for these
women were obviously low-grade fruit that would fall with little
shaking, but this was not a subject to broach with George. He
knew that his partner would not care to discuss his addiction to
fine women and new money, but clearly he was happy, for, these
days, whenever George climbed to his feet it was noticeable that
one buttock was heavily swollen with a roll of dollar bills. Bert

reached over and turned off the bedside lamp. George must live his life according to his own plans, and if this involved his sitting downstairs with a cigar in one hand and a tall drink in the other, and a tan girl on his knee, then so be it. After all, both George and Bob Cole were grown men.

Jimmie Marshall knows that these talented men of keen ambition and prodigious appetites will be the bedrock upon which the future of the race will be built. His charge is not to judge these men but to facilitate them, and give them a place in which they might work and rest and play. He often flicks through the ledger just to remind himself of their vintage. Young men in their twenties, only one or two of them in their thirties. Has there ever been a time when colored America has produced such a roster of talented individuals? Together these colored men of the theater are rewriting the rules of what it means to be a Negro in America, and all of them under his roof, playing their music and singing their songs, spending their afternoons rehearsing, asking for water and juice, discreet about whatever else they might use, and then drinking strong liquor long into the night and satisfying themselves with an ever-changing cast of admirers. There is no blind eye to turn. Jimmie Marshall sees it all, but they know that he will never mention an encounter or a rendezvous to anybody, not even to others among the band of brothers. No, this is not the way to conduct business. Jimmie Marshall understands his clientele, and as long as he respects them, then his hotel on Fifty-third Street between Sixth and Seventh will be their haven and the place from which they will attempt to change America.

Men are already lounging outside of Marshall's, one foot back up against the wall, pulling on cigarettes and tipping their hats to passing ladies. The slow male rhythm of the day. And then they see George's girl and step to one side to let her pass, with a volley of "ma'am's" and "morning's," and up the steps she bounces with a thin grimace on her lips but little else to betray the fact that she does not care for these men or their deportment, for not one of them possesses the breeding to avert his eyes when in the presence of a lady. Once Ada reaches the lobby the smirk buckles on the face of Mr. Marshall. He recognizes her and his hands begin to twitch, and she watches as he clasps them together in front of him. She immediately understands and throws him a weak smile, but no words pass between them. The only question is how to maintain her composure in such circumstances, for clearly neither of them is to blame for this unfortunate turn of events. Ada feels the beads of perspiration pooling in her armpits and then dripping helplessly down the inside seams of her special dress. *Yes ma'am.* Mr. Marshall. Should she call him by his name? *Yes ma'am.* Mr. Marshall, I'd be most grateful if you could tell Mr. Walker that I stopped by to call on him. *Yes ma'am.* Mr. Marshall, when George has finished entertaining would you be so good as to remind him that today we have an appointment? Mr. Marshall, please don't tell him that you saw me. *Yes ma'am.* Mr. Marshall, please don't mention my presence here this morning. Mr. Marshall.

It would be an exaggeration to call it a park, but that's what Lottie called it when she bragged about how her always-attentive Mr. Williams escorted her there to relax. She regaled Ada with stories of how Mr. Williams encouraged her to sit comfortably and then wooed her with tales of his early life, but it would be an exaggeration to call it a park. Two benches set down in a small field of concrete. A queer-shaped quadrant with a single flower bed, but coloreds were permitted to sit in this park in the middle of New York City and contemplate their day, their life, their predicament.

Ada sits by herself, her damp dress clinging to her sides, and she stares at the near-horizontal branches of the solitary tree that suggests that the name "park" might not be a misnomer. One thickset tree, two dozen tired branches, one hidden sun, a city, a roar, confusion raging in her head, and hot tears trapped behind her eyes. One stupid photograph for a tobacconist's advertisement and she throws herself like a cheap bouquet into the hands of a man who carelessly drops her and picks her up and drops her and picks her up again. Of course, it makes sense that every woman should want him, but why can he not learn to say no? Or at least learn to protect her? She would settle for this. Ada has yet to approach George with this idea *(Protect me, George)*, but she knows that she must find these words. With his spats, and his embroidered vest, and his gold teeth, she understands why every woman wants him.

He dreams vividly, and in full color. The powerful images are always captivating, and frequently they overwhelm him with their intensity, but he is unable to arrest his dreams. He often wakes up in the morning, the sheet and pillow soaked with sweat, his body cold and shivering, having tossed and turned all night in the damp bed. Hot sun, that is what he remembers most about the Bahamas of his birth. Hot sun, tall trees, and the sound of the sea, although he cannot remember actually ever going into the water for that would have meant taking off his clothes and already he was conscious of his size, and he had no desire to draw unwanted attention to himself. And so he would sit and listen to the gentle engine of the sea, and occasionally walk on the beach and let the sand funnel through his toes, and he remembers these moments and dreams of his tall stately father, who walks as though he is balancing the roof of the sky on his head, and his mother, with her light skin and strange green eyes, who suggests many worlds in one face. His parents say little to him, but they radiate a quiet authority that is confirmed by the manner in which others look at them. He understands that the pair of them have little money, but they possess a refined quality that he must never betray by behaving like the rough barefoot children from Irish Town or Wendell's Reef, with their backsides hanging out of their pants, children who will never leave the island or visit any place in their imagination. He dreams of the warm tropical Caribbean, and a childhood of few cares or concerns; he dreams of a boyhood blessed with books and sun and sand and long hot days that merge one into the other as though the world will for evermore proceed in a seamless pattern of Caribbean indolence. And then he wakes up in a shapeless sodden patch, his sweat having cooled so that any movement sends chills racing through his gracefully curved body. His hot Caribbean past undermined by cold American anxieties, and his tired mind still spinning backward, trying eagerly to reclaim the Bahamian beach that, all those years ago, his parents gave up for Florida.

He once more closes his eyes and urges his mind to hurry back in the direction of the Caribbean, but this time he finds himself shipwrecked in Florida with the shocked faces of his parents staring at each other, and their son looking intently at the horizon trying desperately to repossess what his family has recently left behind. In this new place they are now encouraged to see themselves as inferior and they are to be paid less than others for picking oranges from the tired branches of row after row of squat trees. In this new place called Florida they are not treated as West Indian people who have come to America by steamship and who are keen to work; they are not viewed as migrants who are prepared to remake themselves in the new American world, but who nevertheless hold fast to a dream that one day they might return home with money in their pockets to live out the late autumn and winter of their lives. In this new place they are simply Negroes. In this new place, young Bert looks at his distraught father, who, unable to face the humiliation of an immediate return to the land they have just waved farewell to, promptly gathers up their belongings, and his eleven-year-old son, and steps on board a ship bound for California, on the far side of this already vexing United States of America.

To his young mind, Panama is simply a narrow strip of water along which the ship moves with dull deliberation. The vessel scarcely deviates to the left or to the right as it furrows a lonely passage across the watery breadth of this uninspiring country before entering the blue water of the Pacific. Whenever he dreams of a sea voyage it is this ship that he is on, his father struck dumb by the knowledge of one American failure and fearful of another in the west. It is on this ship that he develops his fear of water, so much so that long before the ship reaches San Pedro, California, he has already decided that unless it is absolutely necessary he will never again set foot on board such a vessel. And then he notices a thick film of grease on the sea that neither the water will swallow nor the sun burn off, and he looks up and sees the busy Californian harbor with its low flat buildings coming into view, and he turns slightly and the dampness of the bed startles him awake, but he knows that the dream is unfinished and so he rolls in the other direction until he once more discovers sleep and the happier images of his father finding work as a citrus grower, and his mother's relieved face as she takes in people's laundry in their new town of Riverside, California. These visions quickly banish memories of the ship and the water and Florida, and the Williams family now begins to learn how to be both of the Caribbean *and* of the United States of America; they begin to learn how to be coloreds *and* niggers, foreigners *and* the most despised of homegrown sons. Eleven-year-old Bert begins to learn the role that America has set aside for him to play.

"You see, at the age of sixteen I left my Riverside school to join a medicine show. Although my grades were sufficient for there to be talk of my attending Leland Stanford University, where I believe I might easily have found a place and intellectual company, clowning and performing were already a part of my life." He told this to Lottie while they were courting. He confessed to her that it deeply disappointed his father that his son intended to abandon his studies for something as worthless as the stage, but for five years Bert had grown increasingly separate from other boys, who looked at this tall, queerly accented stranger in their midst and found it difficult to know where or how to place him. He was clearly not one of them, and thousands of miles away to the south and to the east was an island about which they knew nothing, and about which they cared even less. And so a somewhat vulnerable Bert, whose size and slick comic wit had saved him from many beatings, left school and joined a crudely assembled medicine show where buffoonery and desperate clowning were the mask behind which he continued to hide, until his young spirit could take no more abuse and he agreed to become a singing waiter at his town's famous Old Mission Inn. However, the multiple indignities of this demeaning role also proved too much for him and so, much to his father's relief, in 1893, the nineteen-year-old colored veteran of the medicine show circuit "retired" from the entertainment business and took a job as a bell-boy at the finest hotel in town, the Hollenbeck. The young Negro was expected simply to tote bags, and he was most definitely not encouraged to elicit any laughter. But the silence troubled the gangly teenager, for to perform—this time as a servant—but to receive neither laughter nor applause in return seemed to him to defeat the whole purpose of the exercise, and in his soul the lanky young boy knew that it would be impossible for him to remain buttoned up for long in the uniform of a hotel bellboy.

Eventually he decided that the misery of the Hollenbeck Hotel, where the verbal insults were often compounded by a swift boot to his seat, or a sharp tug at his jacket, or on one occasion being spat upon, seemed on balance to be no worse than life with the medicine shows, and so, when his former employer pleaded with him to reconsider his premature retirement from the entertainment business, he decided to strip off his bellboy uniform and leave the Hollenbeck, and team up with three white boys and try to make a living touring the lumber camps in the northern extremes of the state. These were rough, wild places where boys who sang and danced were a poor alternative to liquor and women, and these untamed men had no hesitation in letting the youngsters know this. The three white boys would go on first, to test the audience, and then all being well Bert would come onstage for the third song-and-dance number, which would usually bring forth a crescendo of hooting and whistling and more often than not a volley of bottles and the crack of a pistol being discharged into the open sky. The crowd regularly descended into a howling pandemonium, with the reeling white men furiously raining coins at the boys, and their enraged voices screeching vile insults, but the four of them would press on with the show knowing that payment was dependent upon their getting through the whole act. A generous camp owner might smuggle them to a hut and give them a chunk of pie and a place to sleep, but they were often shortchanged and simply told to scoot. Thereafter, they would bunk down for the night in the forest and pray that it wouldn't rain. There were, of course, those nights when his colleagues were offered food and shelter and Bert was left out, but without giving the matter a second thought the three boys stood by him and refused to accept either food or shelter unless the colored boy could share in the spoils. On each occasion the outraged camp owner hastily withdrew his offer to the white boys, which eventually soured the relationship between the four of them for in such dire circumstances it was impossible for the three white boys to hold their resentment at bay. Week after week they struggled from one lumber camp to another, dodging insults and trying to ignore the emptiness in their stomachs. Young Bert began to feel increasingly redundant *and* responsible, and at night he heard them talking and wondering whose idea it was to bring the coon along as the novelty part of their act. Why had their employer been foolish enough to think that the addition of the tall nigger boy would make them special among the scores of other lumber camp troupes who were parading the northern reaches of the west coast? Bert endured long nights in which he listened as the white boys' tempers began to fray, and then unity was finally achieved as they fell into fits of laughter and shared with one another crude imitations of Nigger Bert and his heavy languid singing style while Bert lay "sleeping" under the tall, doomed trees of the lumber camp, all the while trying to shut out these noises of betrayal. And then one morning he shared with them the news that he could take no more of the treatment they were all receiving, and he asked if they would forgive him if he returned alone. The three boys stared at him in astonishment. Guilt caught them unawares, and they pleaded with him that he stay and finish what they had started as a team. Their insincere words disappointed him, but he simply let them know how grateful he was for their support, both now and in the past, yet he insisted that it would be best for everybody concerned were he to leave them to tour by themselves. This time there were no objections and nobody tried to make him stay, but Bert knew that it would be difficult for him to return to Riverside and face his father after this latest misadventure. Desperation sent young Bert to San Francisco's Barbary Coast, where he eventually accepted work as a Hawaiian impersonator singing some of the favorite coon songs of the day, but it was a chance encounter with a member of Martin and Selig's Minstrel Show that changed his destiny. A jet-black nineteen-year-old boy stood with his banjo working the corner of Market and O'Farrell Streets, hoping that he might find a talent to complement his own. Hoping that he might find an end man. Hoping that he might find a friend.

He first sees George in the fall of 1893. The boy is down on his luck, toes poking out of his shoes, backside hanging out of his pants, but he gives off confidence as he tries to scratch a living on the Barbary Coast. This strange boy, who he guesses to be about the same age as himself, is standing on a street corner clutching a banjo and eyeballing all who pass him by. Bert stares at the little man, who looks as though the word "defeat" has been knocked clean out of his vocabulary, and then it occurs to him that if he too is going to be scraping a living he may as well do so in the company of somebody with whom he might talk. But it is George who takes the initiative and touches the imaginary brim of his invisible hat. "They call me George Walker. I'm from Lawrence, Kansas. How about yourself?" He stares down at the short, black man-boy and begins to laugh, at first quietly, but then he loses the shoulders and begins to roar. "So they call you George Walker?" But his new friend isn't laughing. He continues to look down at the short man-boy and he wonders just what kind of banjo-clutching colored creature he has stumbled across. "I'm sorry, Mr. Walker?" He wipes the tears from his eyes with the back of his sleeve, and then he extends a hand. "Pleased to meet you, Mr. Walker. Maybe the two of us should get ourselves acquainted."

An hour later they are still standing together on the corner of Market and O'Farrell Streets. George asks him if he knows where he might smoke out a good end man for Martin and Selig's Mastodon Minstrels, for he explains that he can't go back to Mr. Selig until he finds somebody for the other end. Then, momentarily changing the subject, he leans his banjo up against the wall and volunteers the information that he has made his way out west from Kansas, singing, dancing, and suffering all the degradations of the colored road. Apparently Free Kansas wasn't so free for George, who claims that he arrived in San Francisco penniless, cold, and hungry, but having at least picked up songs aplenty to place on his tongue and having acquired some classy colored strutting for his feet. However, he confesses to having discovered that for a nineteen-year-old colored minstrel boy, the west coast promises little and delivers less, but Bert already understands this.

For over a year the two boys move together, in and out of the city's saloons and variety halls, where they learn to obliterate their true selves on a daily basis. Fourteen hours each day in the California fog masquerading as southern "plantation darkies" or northern "zip coons," rubbing shoulders with Gold Rush dreamers from the Latin, Asian, and European worlds whose own identities appear to breathe free in the misty western air. However, on the Barbary Coast these two boys are expected to perfect clumsy, foolish gestures, and then retire to the wings and silently endure the discourtesy of people mimicking them. Eventually the daily trauma of having to look up to the colored people in the upper balcony and silently beg their forgiveness begins to take a toll on their young spirits. They have both chosen to eschew blackface makeup, which angers most theater owners, but Walker and Williams, with George as the comedian and Bert as the straight man, are now growing weary of trying to be something other than the colored monkeys that the audience in the orchestra stalls assume they are paying to see. For over a year Walker and Williams sing and they dance, and they try not to live down to expectations, and they try not to look up to the upper balcony, and they remain true to their promise that for Walker and Williams, boys onstage dreaming of one day becoming famous men, there will be no blackface makeup.

The Midway Plaisance: I had been told that this place, which was located on Market between Third and Fourth Streets, was formerly known as Jack Cremone's. It was the first melodeon or variety hall in San Francisco to feature hootchy-kootchy dancers (also known as torso tossers or hip wavers), women who were happy to wind and grind and who, the establishment was pleased to note, did not regard their virtue as their chief asset. For ten cents a white man might enjoy the pleasure of watching female entertainment, and for a little more he might enter one of the booths on the mezzanine floor that were protected with a heavy curtain behind which it was understood *private* female entertainment might be procured, the nature of which remained your own business as long as the liquor continued to flow. George and myself performed here, long hard days and nights, from 1:30 p.m. to 4 a.m., as Walker and Williams, providing comic relief to men from the redwood forests who had come to the Barbary Coast to spend a half year's wages on champagne and girls who stuffed banknotes into the lining of their stockings, and who would roll their bellies and bare their bosoms for those rowdy, alcohol-primed men who still had money to spend and who were not yet ready to exchange female pleasures for a good old-fashioned knock-down, drag-out brawl. We performed in this atmosphere with myself as the straight man and George as the comedic banjo picker, each watching the other's back, quick to spot flying chairs or other missiles, determined to earn enough to eat, learning to understand that at best we would be either tolerated or ignored, until it was no longer possible for us to disregard the barking of the drunken audience, who would eventually cry out and demand that the women return, which was our cue to seek temporary refuge in the wings.

Mid-Winter Exposition, 1894: We were anthropological specimens at Golden Gate Park. When the "real savages" promised at the African Dahomeyan village exhibit were delayed en route to America, Walker and Williams were among those who donned animal skins, and through the long hard winter of 1894, and into 1895, we found ourselves close to Africa. We were instructed to impersonate "natives" steaming with perspiration, and we were obliged to kneel before our masters with the clumsy devotion of camels. I worried about George for, despite the discomfiture of our previous engagement, my partner actually missed the noise and the bustle and the girls of the Midway. The simple truth was, something in his spirit was being corroded by being forced to sit in a pen from sunup to sundown and have people stare and point at him. In fact, it soon became apparent that neither one of us could successfully play *primitive*, for there was absolutely nothing in our lives that had prepared us for this demeaning role. I watched as poor George sunk further into depression, and although I too was suffering, *I* chose to dull my pain by studying. At night I consulted John Ogilby's *Africa* and other books on the dark continent, and I read about the place from which my "character" was supposed to have originated. This Dahomey was a West African country, slightly smaller than Pennsylvania, whose coastline gave out onto the Atlantic Ocean. I came to understand that this hot country was mostly flat, with some undulating plains and a few scattered hills and low mountains, and it was a poor place where neither Christianity nor the English language had made much impression. Being in possession of these facts helped me to endure the long days of pretense and shame, but sadly George began to retreat further into himself and we spoke less frequently with each other. And then the Dahomeyans appeared, but it was immediately clear that these bewildered Africans were mystified and unable to comprehend what they were doing in this cold, damp place called America, and so the manager of the exposition made the decision to retain his imposters, who the public seemed able to relate to. He dispatched the Africans back to their "jungle," but George no longer wished to participate and he began to drink excessively, and sometimes he would angrily tear off his animal skin and without warning leave the pen, and I understood that it was time for Walker and Williams to move on and seek fame and fortune elsewhere. As anthropological specimens we had failed.

The two young men share a room down by the water and take turns sleeping on the one narrow bed. Bert lies awkwardly on the floor and looks up at his smaller partner, who pulls deeply on a cigarette and stares at the ceiling. Sometimes George has a detached look about him that suggests he comes from no folks. After all, Bert discovered him on Market Street, just dropped down clear out of the sky. Now life is crushing the pair of them, and they both understand that they need to flee San Francisco, even though this will most likely mean joining a medicine show. George, however, has made it clear to his partner that he is ready to do whatever they have to do, for the city by the bay has nothing more to offer him. In fact, he is desperate enough to consider traveling out to the back of beyond and playing mining towns, places where colored performers generally fear to show themselves, for he understands that unless they act quickly one or both of them are likely to abandon the stage for good. A dejected George lights another cigarette and then returns his gaze to the ceiling, and a worried Bert continues to observe his partner from the vantage point of the floor.

Cripple Creek, Colorado: This small, nondescript town possessed little in the form of government, and the tiny community was under the jurisdiction of El Paso County. In 1890 all of this changed when Gold Fever put Cripple Creek on the map and it rapidly became the fourth-largest gold-producing town in the world. Tent cities sprung up everywhere, and wooden storefronts suddenly lined the dusty streets. The booming town is high in altitude, and none of its forty mines stand below an elevation of nine thousand feet, while some are situated over eleven thousand feet above sea level. This is a tough, volcanic landscape where the dry land is chiseled in rocky ridges and the odd scraggly dwarf tree manages to cling on to a cliff face, but little else flourishes in this first range of the Rockies save mountain grasses, wildflowers, and over five thousand desperate fortune seekers foolhardy enough to have moved eighty-five miles southwest of Denver along wagon-cut roads, and then climbed skyward in the hope of prospecting for new veins by sinking hole after hole into the parched earth. These are crazy times, when a man might arrive on a passenger coach heavy with people, and with nothing to his name but the dusty clothes on his back, and days later the same man might possess the wealth to buy a dozen mansions in any of the fanciest eastern cities. Young Walker and Williams enter Cripple Creek as part of a medicine show, fatigued from days and nights and weeks of rough living, but they still dress well, and they keep their spirits afloat with a high-energy performance that never fails to achieve laughter. But they both know that their chief aim is not to produce laughter but to distract the liquor-filled prospectors so that these desperate and bitter men cannot think clearly about who or what is in front of them. However, here in Cripple Creek, with its newly acquired wealth and its rampant sense of its own importance, the sight of postperformance Walker and Williams in fine clothes causes some prospectors to scratch their heads and think all too clearly about what and who is in front of them and so, at the point of a gun, they strip the fancy clothes from the nigger boys' backs and force Walker and Williams to wrap themselves in burlap sacks before escorting them to the edge of the town. At ten thousand feet, and bereft of jacket, shirt, pants, and shoes, the young performers walk barefoot out of Cripple Creek with laughter ringing in their ears. They understood that going back to the medicine show circuit was always going to be a delicate business, but here in Cripple Creek, Colorado, the two young men finally discover the true extent of the danger and they decide, No more.

He tells her that after Cripple Creek he and George decided to head east. He tells her this as part of his wooing narrative and she listens to her tall, handsome young man who always remembers to bring her flowers. Sitting together on one of the two benches in *their* modest city park, he admits that by the time the pair of them reached Detroit they both realized that they would have to try something new. He pauses and coughs, and then he looks all about them. They like to sit together and feel New York City licking past on either side, marooned in this small quadrant of concrete with the tattoo of horse's hooves filling the silences in their sputtering conversation. He now looks her full in the face as a distant church bell strikes the hour and signals the onset of dusk. In Detroit we made the decision, at Moore's Wonderland Theatre. Again he pauses, but he is careful to make sure that the smile never leaves his lips. He is tense and eager that none should overhear, but there is nobody else in the park. She does not understand. You see, he continues, it made more sense to both George and myself that we exchange roles, so I became the clown and he became the straight man, and right away the laughs came more easily. She watches as he throws back his head and laughs out loud. Walker and Williams became Williams and Walker. You'd never believe it was George, stepping and prancing and throwing everybody those uppity looks, and our immediate success made us wonder why we had never thought of it before. It also made things a little easier between the two of us, although there had never been any real problems, just a little tension from the way things were working out, but it was not anybody's fault, and neither one of us was blaming the other one. He pauses as though he has suddenly revealed too much, and she looks at him but says nothing. His mind is still full and he has not finished. They both know that there is something else. And so, having paused for as long as he dare, he continues. And the makeup. George was not happy but I tried the makeup and became somebody else. She watches his face struggle to hold the smile. The makeup. She places her hand on his arm and squeezes slightly. She understands that he is asking to be forgiven, but he is not an uncouth Ethiopian delineator, nor is he a shouting coon. He is no Ernest Hogan or Bob Cole in crude blackface. She understands that her suitor is a man who is playing a part. He is playing a shuffling, dull-witted, clumsy, watermelon-eating Negro of questionable intelligence. He is playing a character. He is a performer who applies makeup in order to play a part. Sitting in the small concrete park, his large hand now resting lightly on her left knee, she smiles and then decides that the less they talk about Detroit the better it will be for both of them. She takes her small hand from his arm and places it on top of his hand. And then, he says, his hypnotic voice as insistent as waves breaking against the shore, we made our way to New York City and became the Two Real Coons and entered vaudeville, which meant no more medicine shows, no more Barbary Coast or Cripple Creek, we were in New York City doing vaudeville with George's new dandified character and my own impersonation of a Negro. I was now the lazy, slow-footed half of the team, and I had adopted cork. She looks at the beautiful white roses in her lap. He always chooses the finest blossoms and these days her room is forever high with the aroma of freshly cut stems. Although she has said nothing to anybody beyond Ada, everybody knows that a gentleman caller is pursuing the recently widowed Mrs. Thompson, for the scent of flowers permeates the musty air of the otherwise dull boarding-house. Again, he looks across at her. The light is beginning to fade now, but she can see that he is watching her closely as she reaches with her free hand and pulls the shawl closer to her shoulders. A casually draped arm would be acceptable, but she understands that he is not this type of a man. Up above, the wind begins to comb through the solitary tree, and she spies a slither of moon in the darkening sky. I have not talked about the cakewalk, he says. It was George's idea to add the cakewalk to the act for he thought that it would make everything a little more tasteful. He opens up his smile now, and she smiles along with him. She knows all about the cakewalk, for these days everybody does the cakewalk in their act, but only Williams and Walker have the nerve to call themselves the world champions of this elegantly strutting dance and to challenge all comers. Only Williams and Walker possess such a high sense of themselves, but after all, this is why she is sitting right here with Mr. Williams. She admires his spirit, and she is at peace with everything that he has told her. As they fall again into one of their familiar silences, she feels happy that he has shared with her at least one small part of the story of his passage to New York, but already she understands that this man's heart is likely to remain a deep ocean of jeweled secrets, some of which, with time, he may well bestow upon her. As the tree finally fades to black and the streetlights are illuminated, this thought comforts her. But her suitor does not appear ready to leave just yet. He seems to be lost in his own thoughts, and she is reluctant to say anything that might disturb his reverie, and so, despite the cold that is piercing her shawl and tormenting her thin body, and the wind that is threatening to dislodge her small hat, Lottie sits in the gloomy park and says nothing.

"Lottie child, you really want to marry a colored performer? Girl, you scarcely know the man." Ada tightens the straps on her shoes. "Your husband's barely cold, but at least Sam was a businessman. This white man's fool acts like he's better than us, but you and me both know that he ain't no better than any of us, even if people *do* know how to call out his name."

Lottie looks herself up and down in the dressing room mirror, and then she picks up the powder brush. These days she finds it necessary to apply extra makeup, which both depresses and alarms her. She knows that at her age she ought to be thinking of taking up something other than hoofing and clowning, and her late husband always said as much. But what? She pivots and faces Ada, whose exasperated expression makes it plain that there is little point in Lottie saying anything further. Clearly, Ada understands that Lottie's sail is already hoisted, and that she is moving inexorably in the direction of her young man, and this being the case Lottie decides to say nothing and simply finish applying her makeup. Perhaps, Ada should mind her business. Young Mr. Williams never said that he was better than anybody else, but she won't bother to remind Ada of this fact. All young Mr. Williams does is *act* as though he is better than other folks, and this is good enough for her. This has made all the difference.

On the day of the wedding Lottie opens her door and discovers Ada standing before her with one hand planted firmly on her hip.

"Good morning, Ada."

Lottie steps to one side to let her friend pass by. As she does so she smells the perfume and the lavender water that Ada loves to sprinkle about her neck and wrists in a poor attempt to mask the stench of the hair products that Mrs. McDonald from Jamaica sells Ada by the bucketful, foul-smelling creams and ointments that promote the so-called new colored beauty.

"You're not planning on taking a seat?"

Ada sits with a theatrical heaviness that suggests unease. Lottie stares at her friend and then decides that whatever is on her mind, Ada must take responsibility for sharing it. She looks beyond Ada and out through the undraped window at the beautiful fall morning in New York City. This should be a day of joy, but Lottie is being forced to endure the irksome presence of her friend, who now slumps.

"You *sure* you want to marry to this man?"

"Of course I'm sure. I'm thirty-four years old, and nobody ever accused Charlotte Louis Johnson of not knowing her own mind."

A silence descends between them and Lottie feels guilty for having spoken so sharply. She looks at Ada, who is now concentrating on the floor beneath her feet.

"Ada, if you're concerned that I haven't finished my grieving for Mr. Thompson, then you can quit your worrying. Sam was a businessman in all things, including his marriage. He took good care of me, and made sure that I didn't want for anything, but Sam's gone, and I've done my share of lamenting on account of my late husband."

Her friend looks up and meets her eyes.

"Lottie, I only want what's good and right for you, but since I started to see George I noticed something about the both of them. Fact is they're already married to their work. All they ever think about is what they need to do to make Williams and Walker even more famous. I mean, do you think that either of them are really going to lose any sleep troubling themselves over us?"

The street noise begins to rise now as the day matures. She understands that Ada means well, and a part of Lottie wants to reach out and hug her. But on this most special of days what she desires more than anything else is for Ada to wish her unconditional joy and happiness. However, Ada continues to sit marooned in her own circle of frustration and Lottie stares blankly at her friend and tries not to let Ada's words or behavior cloud her second wedding day. She already knows that her husband-to-be is an ambitious man, and she has already discovered that beyond his declarations of affection for her he has difficulty sharing his feelings. But he cares, that much she is sure of, and in spite of Ada's words of caution she believes that the future is theirs for them to make together.

Ada walks briskly up Seventh Avenue, threading her way neatly through the morning rush of pedestrians. She feels guilty for she knows that her visit has unsettled her friend, but after the wedding there will be ample time for her to repair whatever damage she has wrought. Right now she must hurry and collect her new dress. When she reaches Fifty-third Street she looks up at the tracks of iron that stride through the air above her, and then she hears the sound of the train as it thunders its way in her direction. The smooth majestic turn to the east has already taken place on Ninth, and as it now enters the block between Sixth and Seventh it begins to slow down and make ready for the sharp turn south on Sixth Avenue. Ada crosses the street, preferring not to walk beneath the train as its brakes begin to screech. Superstition, she knows, but she backs into a doorway and waits. As the train passes from view the acrid, soot-laden air blows into her face. Fifty-third Street may be the center of colored American life, the main street of black Bohemia, but Ada has never felt truly comfortable on these dark blocks that are shadowed with the latticework of the El.

He slips the ring neatly onto her finger, it requiring neither pull nor push for he has been careful to ensure that it is the right size. Whenever he held her hand he surreptitiously measured her ring finger with the tips of his own delicate fingers, and she smiled imagining that his subtle squeeze was nothing more than that—a subtle squeeze. She angles her face up toward his and he leans down and for the first time he publicly tastes those lips. Cherry. She tastes like cherries, and a smile lights up his face. He raises his eyes and looks across at George and Ada. He is kissing his wife, and on this special day she tastes like cherries and he is happy for he loves cherries.

His marriage surprises the ambitious colored men of Marshall's Lounge, for they never imagined him to be a kinsman who revered women. In fact, nobody can remember a time when they'd ever witnessed him with female companionship, but George, who has known him longer than anybody, refuses to offer up an opinion on the subject even though Bob Cole and Ernest Hogan buy extra drinks and try to encourage him to talk. But George remains steadfastly silent, and the newly married couple move into a large room at the top of the hotel and thereafter pretty much keep to themselves. Sometimes Bert will sit out with George and smoke a cigarette and plan what their next move

might be, and occasionally they are joined by the industrious Will
Cook and his impatient partner, Paul Dunbar. All four of them
believe that legitimate musical entertainment is the way forward
for the colored man, and they spend their days writing songs and
sketches and their nights speculating about the future. An
excitable George will sometimes whisper in his partner's ear that
Cook and Dunbar are the men who are definitely going to rescue
them from the New York City vaudeville circuit, and if they are
ever going to be more than Two Real Coons then they ought to
listen to these men. And so they listen to Dunbar's fiery talk, and
they tune in to the silvery melodies that Cook hammers out on
the piano in Marshall's Lounge, but they are not the only ones
who are paying attention. Bob Cole and Ernest Hogan sit around
with their expensive drinks and their ostentatious cigars, and they
also give ear to Cook's melodies and Dunbar's versifying for
despite the crude limitations of their own minstrelsy they too
have dreams of stardom. Bert is soon convinced that Cook and
Dunbar are indeed the key to their future, and although he has
recently married, he too learns to stay up late. As the men's voices
soar louder with each late-night round of drinks, Bert discovers
how to make his own contribution to the proceedings, adding an
erudite point here or a powerful suggestion there as he stabs the
air with his cigarette. He is avoiding something; they all know it,
but nobody, not even George, will speak of this directly. Together
with Cook and Dunbar, the four men intensify their planning
and arguing, and they squabble over the virtues of the cakewalk,
and which theaters a colored performer ought best to avoid, and
whether coon songs really do bring down the race, and how much
a man can think or feel beyond the mask, but nobody asks Bert
why he is not upstairs with Lottie, who they know regards the
habitués of Marshall's Lounge with a barely disguised contempt.
Bert's world is dividing into two, and it is clear that at some point

a decision will have to be made, but this is his own private business and it has nothing to do with anybody else; not these men, not George, nobody.

She lives now by candlelight, alone, propped up in bed with a book, waiting for her husband to shamble his way upstairs and into a body-warmed bed. She has rekindled her interest in romantic fiction and she understands that in order for her marriage to survive they will have to find a place of their own, far from this hotel, for this man is certainly not levelheaded Mr. Sam Thompson, businessman. She has married a performer, albeit a special kind of performer for her new husband appears to be pained by his profession, but she attributes this anxiety to his having come from the islands. They are a different people, that much she now appreciates, and for them the problem of being colored in America appears to engender a special kind of hurt. But there is something else troubling her husband, a torment that she cannot fathom. At night, in their bed, he recoils from her touch, and his eyes brim with tears at the slightest woe. Now that they are married he calls her Mother, but she does not have the heart to ask him to discover an alternative word for she instinctively understands that he has no other. She would prefer Lottie, or wife, or darling, for Mother instantly reduces her to something less than a woman, but she imagines that in some part of his unconscious this is probably how her husband now regards her. As being something less than a woman, a companion perhaps, or a new extension to the family, but certainly not the trusted bedrock upon which he will build the rest of his life. This one inappropriate word, Mother, speaks to the crisis in both their lives. Reading alone in their room at the top of Marshall's Hotel, she now realizes that she has taken on a new, and onerous, responsibility and perhaps Ada had been trying to warn her about this. As she leans over to blow out the candle it strikes her that despite many years of contented marriage to Mr. Sam Thompson, there *are* things about the souls of men that she has yet to learn; in fact, it is possible that Ada understands men and their ways better than she does. The room plunges into darkness and she admits to herself that it has never crossed her mind that Ada might be better acquainted than her with anything, beyond dancing.

Lottie does not know whether to talk to him about her hair. The fact is she does not talk to anybody about her hair. She simply hopes that nobody will notice. It is her own private misery, and she is seldom without a small hat. Mr. Thompson always chided her about this, and she promised him that she would try to be less self-conscious, but this has not proved possible. When she was a child, the hot iron and grease that her grandmother applied to her scalp produced little change beyond burning her so badly that she felt as though her whole head was a flaming ball of fire. In the years that have followed her hair has remained kinky and knotted and, worst of all, short. As she grew into womanhood she toyed with the idea of a wig, but unable to face the drama of moving between the wig and her natural state, she decided instead to mask the deficiency with a pretty hat. Mr. Thompson used to complain about her wearing a hat indoors, which served only to increase her disquiet, but then he fell silent, which made her feel as though there was tacit approval for her covering up her head. When Mr. Thompson stopped touching her she blamed her hair. She begged her hair *stylist* to find some treatment that would save her marriage, and together they began purposefully to work through all the products on the shelves, but to no avail. And then Mr. Sam Thompson died in Chicago, and Lottie relocated to New York and sought refuge in her less than noteworthy stage career, but the sad failure of her hair seemed to perfectly mirror the bleakness of her life until she accompanied Ada to the photographer's studio where her friend had an appointment to pose for a tobacco company. Sadly, of late, her hair has stopped growing altogether, and the awkwardly sprouting two-inch tufts have become increasingly precious for she now fears their disappearance. Onstage she makes sure that her costumes always call for a bonnet, and this enables her to dance and sing without feeling excessively awkward. However, once she returns to the shared dressing room, she keeps her bonnet tightly fastened to her head and quickly removes her makeup. Having done this she picks up her hat and excuses herself, and only when she is safely secreted in the privacy of the bathroom does she exchange the bonnet for the hat before making her way back to the dressing room, where she knows that eyes are upon her for there is nothing subtle about her transformation. Now that she has remarried the problem of her hair is beginning once again to dominate her mind, so much so that shortly after her wedding she found the courage to ask Ada if she knew of anything that she might do to rectify the situation. While Ada expressed sympathy, she made it clear that if the products that Mrs. McDonald gave her to use on her own hair had no effect on Lottie's, then she was at a loss to know what else to suggest. An embarrassed Lottie lowered her eyes. Clearly Ada had no idea of what it had cost her to confess to this problem, and having done so Lottie felt humiliated.

She blames her grandmother. After all it was she who, after her mother died giving birth to her younger sister, raised the pair of them as her own with the authority of the Lord as the stick to beat them with. From the age of three, when Lottie passed into her grandmother's care, Saturday afternoons were given over to the straightening iron for the following day involved church. And so began the weekly ritual in which a terrified Lottie would be forced to submit to the agony of her grandmother's attempts to tame her kinky head. Everything was about appearances, and her grandmother made it clear that no kin of hers was going to look like they should be walking barefoot. When her sister was less than two years old, she too was introduced to the ritual, but Florence's hair took nice and easy, which only made her grandmother all the more determined to conquer Lottie's head. Florence had "good" hair that flowed out to her shoulders, and inch by inch, her grandmother teased it down her younger sister's back. However, despite years of this tugging and pulling and rubbing and creaming, her own hair remained stubbornly short and knotted. Of course, her resentment of the Saturday afternoon ritual meant that Lottie never truly engaged with the Lord's day, although she could not admit to this. However, what caused her the most sorrow was the fact that over time a chasm grew between herself and Florence. While she could never bring herself to blame her sister for the death of their mother in childbirth, she took exception to the manner in which Florence flaunted her tresses and silently mocked her less fortunate older sister. Their grandmother seemed to delight in reminding them both that Florence resembled their father, with the same light blue eyes and "good" hair, but neither of them knew whether this was true or not for neither sister had ever set eyes on the man. They knew (but *how* they knew they were not sure) that he was a tall, good-looking gambling man from across the river who worked the boats, often going down as far as New Orleans in search of his thrills, and they had also heard the persistent rumors that he had once killed a man. But over the years the gulf between the two sisters grew wide and they seldom spoke about their father, or their mother, or about anything that mattered. As a young girl Lottie sang and danced, which was her way of hiding her wounded self, while Florence simply stood still but seemed pleased with herself that she seemed to be attracting the attention of strutting older boys. Hardly a week passed by without their anxious grandmother taking Florence to one side and chiding her for her wanton behavior, but soon little else seemed to matter to Flo, not church, not her big sister, and certainly nothing that the ailing old woman might say to her. When their grandmother finally died, leaving the two teenage girls alone with nobody to look out for them, Lottie tried to play both mother and grandmother but it was too late. Florence, her hair now down to her waist, had grown as wild as her grandmother had feared, and fast-talking Teddy Washington had already entered her life with his gun-toting, mannish ways. He had long been determined to make young Flo his *woman*, and within a month of their grandmother's funeral the child in Flo's thirteen-year-old belly suggested that Mr. Washington had already succeeded. A year later Lottie took off for Chicago, and a life on the stage, but by then her sister was already carrying her second child and looking ten years older than her true age. Lottie found decent lodgings in Chicago, and a job in a show that presented colored people in a respectable light. She also found a woman who was prepared to take on the challenge of her hair, but after eagerly accepting a great deal of Lottie's money, this woman was ultimately forced to admit defeat. However, some men still found Lottie attractive company and sought her out, but the young dancer was not in any hurry to find herself attached to a husband. She finally kindled an affection for the Lord, and the church became her constant companion until Mr. Sam Thompson began to appear at the theater each evening. After every performance he made a habit of waiting for her by the stage door, but not with plaintive, hopeful eyes like the other men who loitered in the narrow alleyway. This man waited with a silver-topped cane in his gloved hand, and a chin held high, and eyes clear and bright, and a voice so deep it sounded like a train rumbling by.

Eventually Florence had three children, all girls, and all by Mr. Washington, but before the third child declared itself, her beau disappeared and she had no idea if he would ever return to her. To begin with she asked around, venturing into drinking dens that she knew he used, and although she was clearly big with Mr. Washington's child this did not deter wet-lipped men from sidling up to her and offering to make her and her children comfortable. And then it struck her: Teddy Washington must be either dead or in prison for nobody would dare talk to Teddy Washington's girl in this manner if there was even the slightest possibility of his returning. A desperate Florence needed money to put food on the table to feed her two children, plus the one in her belly, but she could not bring herself to write to Lottie, who she heard had just married some swanky colored businessman in Chicago. And so Florence went back to Willie's Foxtrap and asked a balding, thickset nigger sport named Duke the same question that she had asked him the week before, but the man had still not seen or heard from Teddy Washington. This time Florence sighed and looked Duke up and down for she understood that whether she liked it or not she would need the protection of a man, good or bad, if she was going to get through this life. And so, after the birth of Teddy Washington's third child, Duke started to pay her manly attention, running his fingers through her long black hair, and whispering in her ear, and then he too walked clear out of her life, for high-pitched wailing from another man's offspring was not something that he had bargained for. But other men did not seem to mind. They left crumpled bills on the side table before they hit the door and disappeared back onto the streets leaving Flo to endure the resentful eyes of her children, who by now were becoming familiar with the uncomfortable weight of the word "company."

Mr. Sam Thompson broke the news to her late one weekday afternoon. Lottie was sitting in the drawing room readying herself to leave for the theater when Mr. Thompson returned home early from work and sat down opposite her. For the longest while he said nothing, and he simply stared at his wife as though unable to release whatever it was that was dammed up inside of himself. And then he spoke quietly, but with a gravity that was meant to assure his wife that everything was under control. But everything was not under control. Florence was dead. The police had found her in a tenement yard behind the city's most notorious juke joint, with her throat neatly cut and her skirt hoisted up over her shoulders. However, Mr. Thompson spared his wife the more intimate details of her sister's death and remained loyal to the plain facts of the situation. Florence with her good hair was gone, and the three children were being looked after by the city. Mr. Thompson continued, and he made it clear to his wife that should she wish to take in her three nieces, then he would find it in his heart to tolerate the clamor of growing children in his world. But the single word "tolerate" was like a slap in her face, and Lottie immediately smiled and shook her head. Thank you, but she was sure that the children were being properly cared for, and then the tears began to race down her cheeks. Mr. Thompson leaned forward and eased himself out of the chair. He had to return to work.

She hears her new husband walking slowly up the stairs. His footsteps are heavy so she knows that he has drunk a little more than is good for him, but unlike George, he always stops short of getting tongue-drunk. In the case of her husband, drink simply causes him to stumble somewhat, and melancholy to descend. He pushes the key into the door and eases it open before pausing, as though worried that he might be rousing her from sleep. But she is never asleep, for she likes to wait up and make sure that he returns safely, and so she lies perfectly still with her eyes tightly shut. He closes the door carefully so that it does not whine or shriek, and then he turns the key. He can see in the dark—a skill she imagines he has perfected from years of waiting backstage in the wings—and then she feels the weight of his body on the end of the bed, and she listens to his heavy breathing as he leans forward and removes first one shoe and then the other. She knows the routine. First the socks, and then the shirt, and then he will stand and remove his pants, careful to fold them neatly and drape them over the back of a chair, and soon after he will slide into their bed, but there will be no touching. Her new husband will lie next to her on his back and fall smartly into a deep sleep that will be announced by the thunderous rumbling of his snoring. And Lottie will lie next to him and stare at the ceiling and continue to plan their escape from this hotel and the dull routine that is already threatening to choke the life out of their young marriage.

She looks at two houses, both of which are beyond their pockets, and she wonders if this Mr. Nail insists on showing her such extravagant residences because of the manner in which she is dressed. However, the third house is better suited to Mr. and Mrs. Williams's needs and their budget. Williams and Walker's new production, *The Policy Players*, is doing well, but not well enough for her husband to buy this property without her help and so this will be her gift to him. She looks out of the drawing room window onto the broad expanse of Harlem's Seventh Avenue—Negro Broadway—and observes finely dressed colored folks promenading up and down the boulevard. This uptown world is changing, and a tall, four-storey house means that if Mr.

Williams truly does wish to bring his mother and father out from California, then there will be plenty of room right here. Mr. Nail watches and waits until he imagines that whatever thoughts are running through her mind have finally completed their circuit, and then he steps forward. She already has her hand extended in his direction, and he gently shakes it.

"I can just picture yourself and Mr. Williams in a fine home like this."

She looks at his beaming face, but having been married to a businessman she understands that punctuating the transaction with such small talk is merely part of the routine.

"Believe me, Mrs. Williams, it is only a matter of time before this whole area boasts the finest-quality colored people."

He places both of his hands behind his back, pushes himself up and onto the balls of his feet, and then rolls forward.

"You know, I do not care to employ the word 'fashionable' because such a word suggests that things may soon change. You are, of course, familiar with the old saying 'Fashions come and fashions go.' The word sounds a little insubstantial to me, if you understand what I am saying."

She does understand what he is saying, but she chooses to say nothing further to this man who seems to care little that he is wasting his time. After all, their business is already concluded. The price is fixed and agreed upon. Why is he still nervously running his untrustworthy mouth in this way? They move deftly down the steep steps and onto the sidewalk. Her mind is made up. She will stroll south as far as 110th Street and the park and then ride a streetcar. Mr. Nail walks six blocks with her and then stops, claiming that he has other clients with whom he is expected to rendezvous. He doffs his hat and politely bids her farewell, and she watches him turn to the left and her eyes follow this man until he is swallowed up by the pedestrian traffic on

West 129th Street. Lottie continues south, walking slowly and with as much proprietorial elegance as she can muster, happy in the knowledge that these fine streets will soon constitute her new vicinity.

He takes the news of the house calmly, as though determined to conceal his true feelings from his wife, but these days so much of his behavior falls into this pattern. They seldom exchange more than the occasional sentence, but he eventually looks up at her as though he wishes to say something. She watches his face struggle with the emotions, but finally there is peace and just two words, "thank you." She asks him if he would like to see the house, or if he would prefer to look at a selection of different properties before signing away their future in this manner, but he simply smiles and tells her that he is grateful that she has taken care of this problem and that he looks forward to the day when they might move out of Marshall's Hotel and into their own residence. He pauses. "Thank you, Mother." His voice falls now to a whisper. "Thank you." Clearly he has said all that he is capable of saying. There is a performance tonight, and she convinces herself that her husband is simply conserving all of his energy for the cakewalking contest at the end of the evening. She rubs and then squeezes the nape of his neck with her gentle fingers. "Would you like me to meet you at the theater after the show?" He smiles again, clearly grateful that she is paying him so much attention, but he shakes his head. "No, Mother. Thank you, but there is no need. I will be fine."

He falls heavily as he climbs the stairs to their large room at the top of Marshall's Hotel. She sits bolt upright in bed and then leans over and lights the candle. She can hear him groaning, but she knows instinctively that it would be improper to get out of bed and witness this spectacle, and so she waits until she hears him drag himself up from the stairs and noisily begin to put one foot in front of the other. She fears that it isn't just the thought of moving and taking possession of a four-storey house that is punishing her new husband like this. In fact, of late, she has begun to wonder if perhaps his parents put the child in him down too early, thus causing him to labor under what appears to be the burden of excessive responsibility. Again she hears him stumble, and this time she rises from the bed and pulls on her gown, but by the time she reaches the door he is already there, bent double, key poised, his pleading eyes looking up at her. Please don't be angry with me, Mother. There are things going on in the basement of my twenty-eight-year-old soul that I cannot talk about. And George does not understand, brimming as he is with a brashness that makes white men angry and causes colored men to move a little closer to him in the hope that some of his confidence might ease its way out of his short dark body and into their own cautious hearts. But me, they look at me and wonder, Mother—they look at me and wonder why I am what I am. All of this with his eyes alone, and she reaches out and takes his hand and key together, and helps his drunken body across the threshold and sits him down on the end of the bed so that the springs squeal and then fall silent again. She leans forward and gently eases off his shoes. Tomorrow, she says, I'll show you the house. Four storeys looking out on to Seventh Avenue just above 135th, and it has a grand entrance, and once you pass inside you'll see there's plenty of room for all of us. He looks at Mother and moves his shoulders first one way and then the other so that she can slip off his shirt. Your folks can come from California. Don't you think it's about time they met your wife? She smiles as she says this, and then she runs a heavy hand back through his nice suite of hair. This really is a capital second husband that she has found for herself, a man solid like a tree but with the sensitivity of a boy. His partner, George Walker, was no doubt downstairs in Marshall's Lounge waiting for whatever clench-waisted, high-yellow dancing girl happened by this evening, but he is Ada's cross to bear, not hers. She knows that a colored woman cannot expect too much out of this life, but Lottie is satisfied with her young man. She has no complaints.

A fatigued-looking Bob Cole passes George the bottle. He waits for him to take another drink before he says anything further. George pours a full glass and then he throws it back in one movement, head, neck, glass, whiskey, all moving as one. George breathes a long sigh of relief and then pours a second glass and passes the bottle back to Cole, who laughs.

"Long night?"

George laughs. "*A Lucky Coon* ain't so lucky for this coon."

Cole pours himself a drink. "Everything all right with Bert?"

"Why you asking?"

"Well you know, since he got married, he's been acting kind of different."

George sits upright and looks at Cole. "Ain't no way to talk about Bert."

Cole opens his broad mouth, ready to insist that he isn't talking about Bert no way, but George holds up his hand.

"Bert got pressures on him that you and me don't fully understand."

Cole laughs sarcastically, but he will not meet George's blazing eyes.

"I said he got pressures on him that maybe we don't understand, and if you can't be respecting this, then maybe it's best you hold your tongue."

Cole is stung now. He has no desire to argue, yet here he is fighting with old George. He takes a drink, and then he turns and addresses his fellow performer with melancholy coursing through his voice.

"I'm just worried, George. Bert ain't never been one to mix in, you know that better than anybody, but this marriage thing seems to have beaten up on old Bert."

George says nothing. He takes a sip of his whiskey and he continues to look closely at Cole, whose face is as easy to read as that of a clock.

Later.

"George, you have to treat women like you're a dead-swell coon who's always got somebody that you're ready to replace them with. You let a woman know that you're feeling too much for her, then it's over for you as a man. You may as well take up with one of those goddamn inverts that you see all over our business. You listening to me, George?"

There were no colored girls in any of the venues they played on the Barbary Coast, and so after their performances George would rush down to the seaport, and the colored taverns, where he knew that a sporting welcome always awaited "Mr. George." "Ladies, if it ain't Mr. George paying us a visit this evening." "Sit yourself down here, Mr. George, you sweet thing you." George was barely out of his teens, but hustling was in his blood and the powdered and overscented dusky belles of the San Francisco seaport recognized one of their own kind. To begin with Bert would accompany him, but while George hurried upstairs in search of company his cautious colleague would stay downstairs by the bar, listening to the piano playing and concentrating on the drink in front of him. When George came back down he inevitably found his friend still there. Sometimes, the barman aside, Bert was the only patron left in the place, and although George was puzzled by

Bert's reluctance he already knew that this was a subject that it was best not to raise with him. And then George began to leave the Midway Plaisance without waiting for his partner, who he sensed was deliberately taking his time in an effort to avoid the seaport. And sure enough some tension between the two of them began to dissipate, for there was no longer any expectation, and some nights Bert even found his way to the seaport by himself. Stumbling downstairs, his shirttail flapping outside his pants, George was always happy to see Bert sitting at the bar and grinning in his direction. And then one night, having taken a good fill of liquor, George forgot himself and asked Bert the question.

"What's the matter, Bert, you don't like catting for women, or you don't like colored girls, which is it?"

Bert looked at him in fake surprise and arched his eyebrows.

"Ain't no other type of girl that I know of."

"Well I know some of these colored girls are sweet on you. And they got moist thick lips like they be putting soft rubber all over your body."

Bert laughed. "I already caught enough hell in my life and I ain't got no interest in catching nothing else."

"You ain't never heard of protection? It's true that some of those female diseases gets ideas and likes to ease their way into a man's body so we all got to be careful."

Bert smiled and shook his head, and then he took another mouthful of his whiskey. "First time I ever went with a girl I guess I wasn't careful."

George tucked his shirt into his pants then leaned back and began to roar with laughter.

"Man, bad luck sure knows where to find you. The first time?"

His friend nodded and took another gulp of his whiskey. Then he turned and looked George full in the face.

"These womenfolks are a strange breed. But I guess you already got that figured out."

George was halfway out the window when the man finally broke down the door and burst into the bedroom. George had one foot on the complex iron labyrinth of the fire escape and one foot marooned in the bedroom when, for some reason, he looked again at the man's wife, who pulled the sheet up to her neck with melodramatic haste. For a moment it occurred to George that his blond conquest might actually be enjoying this drama, and then she screamed and George saw that the irate man had whipped out a pistol from some part of his person and he was pointing it directly at him. He heard the noise of the pistol before he felt the hot pain in his arm, and again the man's wife screamed. George discovered himself on the sidewalk running, and although the husband didn't fire again he knew that the humiliated man was standing above him and watching. It was only when he reached their lodgings, and began to pound vigorously on the door to Bert's room, that George realized that he was light-headed and he was unable to prevent himself from slumping heavily to the ground. He peeled back his jacket and saw that his shirt was covered in blood, but he already understood that there would be no time to call for a doctor. His partner opened the door and peered down at a prostrate George who was trying to smile, but the pain was clearly cutting him like a knife.

"We got to leave Cleveland tonight, Bert."

Bert helped his friend to his unsteady feet and into the room, and he pushed the door shut behind him.

"What happened, George? We got to find you a good colored doctor. Looks like you already lost a lot of blood."

George collapsed onto a chair and shook his head. "Gonna lose a whole heap more if we don't get the hell out of Cleveland."

Bert handed his friend a damp cloth with which to stanch the wound.

"We have to find you a colored doctor on the way out of town. You hear me?" George nodded, his face now knotted in pain. "That white woman's husband catch up with you?"

George looked up at his partner, but Bert already knew the answer to the question.

Detroit, 1896: And the first time he looked at himself in the mirror he thought of the embarrassment and distress that this would cause his father and his heart sank. Down through his body like a stone, down toward those long, oversized boots that announced him as a clown. How could a West Indian do such a thing to himself? The first time he looked in the mirror he was ashamed, but he understood that his job was to make people laugh so they did not have time to ridicule or hurt him. And so he made the people of Detroit laugh. No longer Egbert Austin Williams. He kept telling himself, I am no longer Egbert Austin Williams. As I apply the burnt cork to my face, as I smear the black into my already sable skin, as I put on my lips, I am leaving behind Egbert Austin Williams. However, I can, at any time, reclaim this man with soap and water and the rugged application of a coarse towel. I can reclaim him, but only later, after the laughter. As he looked at himself in the mirror he knew that he had disappeared, and he understood that every night he would have to rediscover himself before he left the theater. The first time he looked at himself in the mirror the predicament was clear, but just who was this new man and what was his name? Was this actually a man, with his soon-to-be-shuffling feet, and his slurred half speech, and his childish gestures, and his infantile reactions? Who was this fellow? Sambo? Coon? Nigger? However, the audience never failed to recognize this creature. That's him! That's the nigger! He looks like that. And that's just how he talks. And he walks just like that. I know him! I know him! But this was not Egbert Austin Williams. This was not George Walker. This was not William E. B. DuBois. This was not Booker T. Washington. This was not any Negro known to any man. This was not a Negro. And the first time he looked in the mirror his heart sank like a stone for he knew that this was not a man that he recognized. This was somebody else's fantasy, and unless he could make this nobody into somebody, then he knew that eventually his eardrums would burst with the pain of the audience's laughter. The first time he looked at himself in the mirror his heart sank. In Detroit in 1896.

It was in Detroit that he first persuaded a disapproving George that this might be a good idea. It was in Detroit that he first betrayed his father. It was in Detroit that he first pushed his hands into the pot and worked the oily substance onto his fingertips. There was a moment's hesitation as he felt the cork slither between his delicate, oversized fingers, and then he began to smear his warm face with the cold potion. Only when he was sure that it was spread evenly across his face did he dare look up and stare into the mirror. He needed to make sure that the edges of the makeup met his hairline. He needed to give himself a consistent tone of blackness, and then he drew on his lips so that they grew beyond his own, swimming out toward his cheeks and down his chin. His lips were the final touch. He erased himself. Wiped himself clean off the face of the earth so that he found himself staring back at a stranger.

The irate woman bursts into his dressing room without knocking and she noisily demands her money. A surprised George looks up at her.

"You finished already?"

The woman holds out a purple-gloved hand and snorts. "Finished what, child? You better talk with that man."

George pulls a thick roll of bills from the back pocket of his street pants.

"Five dollars is what we agreed on, right?"

She takes the money and tucks it into her notebook, all the while pursing her lips in disgust.

"You said you wanted me to do something special for him seeing as he's acting all lonesome and everything, but you better let that boy know that we Detroit girls don't appreciate you out-of-town boys acting in this fashion toward us. He don't want something this fine, then his ignorant ass only needs to say so. No need for the man to be running off his mouth in my face like I ain't nobody. I deserve some mannerly treatment, don't you think?"

George looks the tan girl up and down and slowly a smile breaks out on her face.

"Sugar, I like how you is looking at me. Give me two dollars more and you can taste what your partner didn't want." George laughs and turns from her. "You know," she begins, her voice now shrill with anger, "the two of you all deserve each other. Coming into my town like you all is big and mighty but you ain't nothing but a pair of broke-down little boys masquerading as men."

She slams the door as she leaves, and a resigned George shakes his head. He knows that his partner will be sitting by himself in his dressing room, furious with George for having arranged for a girl to visit with him. But the truth is he couldn't think of anything else that he might offer Bert to help him out of his depression. For the past week, since he began to use the cork and play the simpleton to George's straight man, his mood has clouded over, which makes no sense for despite George's unhappiness with Bert making a blackfaced coon of himself he has to admit that they are now making more coin than they ever did. But Bert is struggling with what he calls his "new character," and George had hoped that a girl might help. She was a gift, a present. He had not meant to anger his friend.

Ada looks around the spacious apartment at 107 West 132nd Street and she hopes that George will appreciate it. Afternoon light streams in through the large undraped windows and a perturbed Ada convinces herself that this is a good place for her to begin to make a home for herself and George. Bert and Lottie have already moved out of Marshall's Hotel, and Ada has now decided that she and George will follow them uptown to Harlem. Somewhat reluctantly George has agreed to marry her, but Ada remains optimistic for she understands the seasonal changes that can quickly, and unpredictably, affect the spirits of men. She knows that George will still keep a room at Marshall's, although he will not tell her, but Ada is determined and she will simply pretend that she knows nothing about George's room, and she will quietly absorb the humiliation and wait patiently until the wind changes direction.

The girl waits for him by the stage door, a slender nymph whose young body looks like it could never support the weight of an overcoat. As he approaches the girl steps forward to block his path and George stops.

"It's your child, Mr. Walker. I'm asking you, please, you have to do something to help me."

George looks rapidly about himself. "Not here," he hisses. "Not here where people can see."

The girl touches his arm, her top lip quivering and water in her eyes. "Mr. Walker, I know you're serious with the dancing lady. Everybody knows that. I seen you together with her and I ain't fixing to make things difficult for anybody. But it's your child, Mr. Walker and I need me some help."

George looks at the girl, who has at least shown the good sense to steer clear of Marshall's. He remembers her, and the disturbing cesarean zip that marks her stomach. He will help her, but she will have to wait until after the weekend. Between now and then he is occupied with plans for his wedding.

Bert soon learns to walk the twenty paces from his door to Metheney's Bar. At first people try to talk to him for he is, the pastor aside, the best-known colored man in the neighborhood. However, they soon recognize that he is not a talking man and so they let him be. Metheney's is a place for men who are serious about their drinking and their solitude. This is not a place for playing numbers, nor is it a place for bragging, or cursing, or womanizing. In Metheney's, king alcohol makes no man sing. A man comes to Metheney's to be by himself, and none more so than Mr. Williams, who sits on an undersized wooden chair at a small brown table in the far corner. There is just one chair, to prevent people from making a mistake, and as he leans forward light from the street spills over Mr. Williams's hunched shoulders and splashes down onto the table and into his tumbler of whiskey. The barman is both tall and broad, with a roll of fat at the back of his neck. He scratches at his stubbled face, dragging a finger, like a plump brown matchstick, across his cheek and down toward the apex of his chin. Later, when Metheney wakes up and comes down to replace him, the barman will go to his rooming house, but only after he has visited the barbershop and encouraged the man to scrape off the fur with a dull razor. He will leave Mr. Williams alone, but he will make sure that the man's glass is full before he steps out and onto Seventh Avenue. Right now he watches the local celebrity, who always sits by himself. Sometimes

Mr. Williams brings in one of his seemingly endless supply of books to read, but most of the time he just sits and smokes cigarette after cigarette, his noble head clouded in tobacco. At the end of the day Bert needs time to think about what he is doing. He needs time to consider and reconsider everything that he has done, and to turn his short life over in his mind and think and drink and drink and think for there is nobody with whom he cares to talk. Not George. Not Mother. He sits and thinks and drinks by himself and colored people respect the fact that this is his way. He remembers the first time he played with a crudely assembled white medicine show out west. Waiting in the cold outside a restaurant that it was impossible for him to enter alone, hoping that a fellow performer from the company might walk by and say, "Hello, young Bert! What are you doing here?" Maybe walk in with him and give him a chance to make himself at home. But nobody came by. Back in those days, Christian charity seemed to be forever in short supply. He takes another long drink and signals to the barman for a refill. The man always offers to leave the bottle on the table for him, but Bert understands that it would not be right. After all, he would not want to disappoint his father. A nervous crease of a smile wrinkles his lips whenever he thinks of his father, way back across the country in California. He watches the barman push the stop back into the top of the bottle, and he notices that the man's face is rough with stubble. Most likely he'll soon visit a barbershop where talking is encouraged and easy topics are pursued with vigor. The many ways that a colored man might prevent himself from contracting syphilis. Whether skin-lightening creams really do work. Whether a plate of tripe fried in batter with hot biscuits and bacon on the side beats out a night spent removing silk slips and panties from a whole harem of willing young ladies. He watches the barman move back behind the bar, and then he looks closely at the other solitary drinkers, who all seem to relish this quiet place that throws them back upon themselves. Funny, he thinks, what men will do to release themselves from the burden of human companionship.

Metheney's opens at noon, every day except Sunday. First, Clyde D unlocks the door and then he steps back so that the smell of the previous evening can pass him by and hurry on down the street. When it is good and gone he enters the gloom, knowing full well that Metheney will be upstairs sleeping off the night before. The man has never learned how to do much of anything except turn off the lights and stagger in the direction of the stairs, but sometimes he is carrying too much liquor to even manage this and he makes a bed of the floor. Once Clyde D came in early and found one of Metheney's wooden-faced whores pushing bottles of liquor into a bag and ready to make her getaway. Clyde D looked down at the floor and he could immediately see that old Metheney was passed out cold. He imagined that the girl had already stuffed Metheney's takings into her pocketbook, having previously slipped something into Metheney's gin so that he wouldn't hear nothing, or know nothing, and now it was down to Clyde D to put his unwashed morning self between the girl and the door and take back the man's money. Keen to avoid a beating, the frightened girl suddenly offered Clyde D what rightfully appeared to belong to any man who was hungry enough to take it, but Clyde D recoiled from the sour bursts of her breath in his face, and then he snatched back the money and the liquor, before pushing the girl out into the street and setting about his business. After first sweeping the floor (careful to avoid Metheney), and then pushing back the tables and dropping the chairs into place, he stepped behind the bar, where empty bottles and filthy glasses were lined up and ready for his attention. Metheney stirred and rubbed a gnarled hand into his face and then, without saying a word, he dragged himself to his unsteady feet and lurched in the direction of the wooden staircase, which groaned under his weight. Mercifully, this morning, Metheney is already upstairs, no doubt still asleep, with his mouth wide open, and sprawled across one of his girls who specialize in late-night secondhand love. The first customers of the day usually wander in while the bar top is still sopping wet from Clyde D's having wiped it down, and they take up their silent seats and order without having to say a word. During the early-afternoon hours it is best not to make too much noise, for Metheney does not like to be roused from his slumber, but there is usually little danger of this for Metheney's is not a talking kind of place.

By the time the evening regulars start to come in off the street, Mr. Williams is usually ready to leave. After all, for Mr. Williams, Metheney's is little more than a fleet detour on his way back home from midtown business. However, on the days that he must perform, Metheney's is a place that Mr. Williams might wander into for a late-afternoon drink before returning home to change his clothes. Before he leaves he looks up and sees two men in wide-brimmed hats who nod in his direction as they enter the premises, and then they respectfully ignore him. They watch as Clyde D reaches over and places their drinks before them, and they grope at the drinks without so much as a hint that they have a tongue in their now unshod heads. Eyes drift upward to where Metheney is now stirring himself, his clay feet banging against the floor as he lumbers to the corner and urgently relieves himself into an enamel pot so that the noise of the piss echoes like rain on a tin roof. This is all part of Metheney's routine, and if he happens to have company, then Metheney's clay feet will move more eagerly back in the direction of the bed, and at first slowly, and then with more vigor, the whole structure of the ceiling will begin to shake as the boss attempts to finish off what he had started the night before. Eyes return to drinks that are now levered toward open mouths. All is right with the world. Clyde D knows that soon it will be time for him to be replaced by Metheney, and he looks across as Mr. Williams slowly pushes his long frame upright. He can tell by the languorous way that he moves that tonight the local celebrity will be onstage in midtown. Tonight Mr. Williams will be a star on Broadway, a man whose pitiable gait is to be applauded. Shylock Homestead in Williams and Walker's production of *In Dahomey*, telling a few hapless jokes and doing a little plaintive singing and some clownish dancing. But that will be later. Clyde D watches Mr. Williams closely and can see that the performer's veins are already buzzing with the dull grandeur of whiskey. Mr. Williams stands tall in Metheney's and reaches for his hat, and all eyes look up and silently bid him his daily farewell. They watch as he moves with deliberation toward the door, and as he opens it Manhattan rushes in to meet them, and then he shuts Metheney's weather-beaten door behind him and all eyes return to the task in front of them. It will be a long night.

The short walk home generally sobers him up, but during the past weeks these few dozen steps have become inexplicably difficult for this thirty-year-old man. Once upon a time he would close the door behind him and pull his jacket tight before setting forth with confidence. The harsh late-afternoon light, and the noise from the street, usually put the edge back into his mind, but these days he often wanders aimlessly, consumed with a fear that tonight, in front of hundreds of strangers, he might lose his way. The few dozen steps have multiplied, and he frequently discovers himself in unfamiliar streets gripped with a sudden panic that he might now be late for his onstage appointment. It sometimes occurs to him that he should walk directly to the theater, but he knows that his wife would not like this. She always insists that he clean up and change out of his relaxing clothes before making his appearance at the stage door, and he does not like to argue. But people notice him walking, with a vertical plume of smoke climbing from his cigarette up toward the sky. They can see that these days his few dozen steps are taking him all over the neighborhood, but nobody feels free to talk to him, not even the pushcart man who dusts his fruit with an old brush and each day is tempted to offer an overripe peach or a bruised apple to the weary-looking Negro. When he returns home, Mother looks the other way and he understands that once again he has failed her.

He finds it difficult to achieve any peace in this new house, but he does not complain to Mother. When troubled he simply pulls on his coat and picks up his hat and he walks the twenty paces to Metheney's and sits by himself. *In Dahomey* is doing well, and he and George continue to collaborate with Mr. Jesse Shipp, with whom they are working hard to sharpen up every aspect of the show. Theirs is the first all-Negro production on Broadway—real Broadway—and everybody is talking about it. Bob Cole and Ernest Hogan are jealous, but even *they* are talking. Everybody is talking. Just thirty years of age and he is starring in a musical show on Broadway. What more could he want?

Only this morning, he and George, together with Mr. Shipp, made some minor changes to the script of *In Dahomey*. The two stars remembered everything they could from the time when, back in San Francisco, they were encouraged to impersonate Africans. They talked endlessly to Mr. Jesse Shipp about their memories of these Africans, about how they walked and how they talked, and Mr. Shipp made notes and promised to add these new elements to his script. *In Dahomey*, starring Williams and Walker. Two real coons. Beyond the corner of Market Street. Beyond the Midway Plaisance. Beyond Cripple Creek. Married men in New York City, nurturing their dreams, but Bert longed to ask George about his dreams for he wondered if his partner shared his own obsession with journeying. He did once ask George if he had ever been on a ship and George simply laughed and poured them both another drink. They were on a Pacific Union train at the time, and through the window they could both see a horizon that was ragged with low mountains. "A ship?" exclaimed George. "A colored man like me don't need no ship when I've got this whole wide country to roam free in." But this was before gold-toothed George was beaten by the rabble, and thereafter began to noisily proclaim what they both already knew to be true, that America wasn't so wide and free after all. For a colored man, that is.

They were hunting Negroes like you might pursue wild game, running up the avenues from south to north with sticks and bottles in their hands. It was merely another of those New York City nights when one small incident in a tavern or saloon sparked a response out of all proportion to the original event. Meanwhile, Bert remained hidden in his dressing room, the theater manager having barred the doors and turned off all the lights in the building. "You'll be safe in here, Mr. Williams," he said. "Shouldn't be any problems for you in here." And so Mr. Williams remained hidden inside the theater, and he was forced to listen to the ugly cacophony of the mob breaking glass and colored bones all over the city. George had already left the building, refusing to exercise any caution, scornful of such behavior. George was on a streetcar that was halfway up Sixth Avenue when three men recognized his *immodest* clothes, and then his well-groomed face, and they dragged the grinning nigger from the vehicle. "Walker!" The name began to be chanted by the hoodlums. "Walker!" "Walker!" Helpless to protect him, a half dozen horrified coloreds stood forlornly in the street and looked on, and then they parted like the Red Sea, forming an unfortunate path along which more ruffians were able to funnel their way toward the object of their hatred. "Walker!" They beat him with fierce blows until he fell over and bundled himself into a small ball, tucking his head down into his chest and protecting it on both sides with his folded arms.

George tries to open his eyes. One real coon. They have broken something, that much he is sure of, for he can feel that things are no longer in line. He will have to wait for help, but then again he is not in any hurry. He is just trying to get to his room at Marshall's. Nothing wrong with a colored man enjoying some relaxation after a hard night's work on Broadway. But tonight his fellow white citizens are angry, and although they have now abandoned him he can still hear their discordant and unruly clamor. And a half dozen blocks to the south, Bert hides in his dressing room with the lights out, his makeup already removed, his street clothes hanging neatly from his broad shoulders, ready to leave whenever America is ready to receive him. Ready to make his entrance without his makeup. But in the meantime he will wait until the theater manager informs him that his audience is ready for him. Then, and only then, will he be able to leave his dressing room.

The man from Dahomey stands in front of him and stares in disbelief. He looks at the mottled animal skin that is draped over Bert's shoulder. He looks at the Indian axe that is tucked into Bert's waistband, and at the headdress fashioned out of old leaves and pieces of twisted twig, which makes it appear as though Bert is wearing a crown of thorns. The man from Dahomey looks at the Chinese lettering that has been painted onto Bert's face, and at the small Swiss bells that are strung together on a fraying piece of string and tied loosely around his ankles, but he says nothing to the American man about this costume. So this is America standing tall and proud before him. It never crosses his mind that this bizarre-looking man could possibly be representing Africa, let alone Dahomey, and against his better judgment the African begins to feel sorry for Bert. The man from Dahomey stands in front of Bert and stares in disbelief at this pitiful apparition and he worries about this strange land called America.

And then one morning Bert and George and the six others who are paid to dress in animal skins gather together, for the manager of the exposition wishes to address them. The gray-bearded man steps from his office and tucks his fingers into the pockets of his vest. Presumably they are now to hand back the skins and bells and axes, for after all it has been clearly understood that their engagement was to be temporary. It was to last until the Africans completed their journey from Dahomey and reached California, and now the Africans are here, and the prospect of unemployment is once again staring these eight young men in the face. The manager of the exposition begins to speak. They have done well and they are popular, but the problem is that the newly arrived savages don't appear to be acclimating to the weather, or to the food, or to the customs. It is going to be too difficult to effectively season them and so they will soon be sent back to where they came from. Would these eight young impersonators of the dark continent be able to stay on for a few more weeks? As he makes his request he smiles and tugs at his vest, as though particularly pleased with himself.

. . .

He watches the Africans gather up their belongings and make ready to leave. There are a dozen of them, all men except two young women. He notices that they all walk slowly on bare, noiseless feet, and they seldom lift their eyes, as though stricken with some form of malady. The man who stood before him is clearly their leader, for they look to this man for guidance yet none among them ever approach him too closely. Evidently, they are tired, and Bert can only imagine how torturous their journey from Africa must have been. He too has suffered the tedium of a journey on a ship, but he understands that his own passage does not compare to the difficulties that these Africans must have endured. And then to finally arrive in San Francisco, only to discover that they are not wanted, and now they are being dismissed without payment, and they face the painful prospect of a long passage back to West Africa. No wonder they move slowly and without enthusiasm. Their lives have been arrested, and now they must return home empty-handed. And with how many promises broken? Nineteen-year-old Bert stands barefoot with a mottled animal skin draped over one shoulder, and he watches the melancholy men and women of Dahomey prepare for their departure.

IN DAHOMEY

1903

Jesse A. Shipp (1869–1934), book
Will Marion Cook (1869–1944), music
Paul Laurence Dunbar (1872–1906), lyrics

A Negro Musical Comedy

PROLOGUE

Time: Three months before beginning of play
Place: Dahomey

CHARACTERS

Je-Je, a Caboceer	CHARLES MOORE
Menuki, messenger of the king	WM. ELKINS
Moses Lightfoot, agent of Dahomey Colonization Society	W. BARKER
Shylock Homestead, called "Shy" by his friends	BERT A. WILLIAMS
Rareback Pinkerton, Shy's personal friend and advisor	GEO. A. WALKER
Cicero Lightfoot, President of a Colonization Society	PETE HAMPTON
Dr. Straight . . . in name only, street fakir	FRED DOUGLAS
George Reeder, proprietor of an intelligence office	ALEX ROGERS
Henry Stampfield, letter carrier, with an argument against immigration	WALTER RICHARDSON
Me Sing, a Chinese cook	GEO. CATLIN
Hustling Charley, promoter of Get-the-Coin Syndicate	J. A. SHIPP
Leather, a bootblack	RICHARD CONNORS
Officer Still	J. LEUBRIE HILL
White Wash Man	GREEN TAPLEY
Messenger Rush, but not often	THEODORE PANKEY

Dancing in the Dark

Pansy, daughter of Cecilia Lightfoot, *in love with Leather*	ABBIE MITCHELL
Cecilia Lightfoot, Cicero's wife	MRS. HATTIE MCINTOSH
Mrs. Stringer, dealer in forsaken *Patterns, also editor of fashion* *notes in* Beanville Agitator	MRS. LOTTIE WILLIAMS
Rosetta Lightfoot, a troublesome *young thing*	ADA OVERTON WALKER
Colonists, Natives, etc.	

ACT I

SCENE I

(Public Square with a house doorway. Above the door is a sign: "Intelligence Office." A crowd is assembled around a medicine show pitchman. Applause at rise of curtain. A banjo player acts as interlocutor as Tambo and Bones tell one or two jokes. The banjoist sings a song. Dr. Straight, the pitchman, addresses the crowd.)

DR. STRAIGHT   After listening to great attempts at beautiful strains of melodious music and pyrotechnical display of humorous humorosities, quintessence of brevity rather than prolix verbosity will best accomplish the purpose for which I appear here this evening. Now that I've made everything so plain that even a child can understand, I'll proceed with business. I hold in my hand a preparation made from roots, herbs, barks, leaf grasses, cereals, vegetables, fruits, and chemicals warranted, by myself, to do all that I claim, even more. I'm not here to sell this article but simply to advertise the greatest boon that mankind has ever known. I will forfeit one thousand dollars to—hold up the money so that they can see it *(Attendants hold up a large sack marked $1000)*— or I will take the same amount from any dark-skin son or daughter of that *genius* Africanus that I cannot immediately transform into an Apollo or Cleopatra with a hirsute appendage worthy of a Greek goddess.

VOICE *(interrupting)* Look here, Mr. Medicine Man, if you 'specs to sell any of dem bottles of whatever you've got there to anybody in this crowd, you'd better bring your language down to the limitations of a universal understanding. I've been standin' here ten minutes trying to figger out what you're talkin' about and I tell you as the old maxim says, "Patience ceases to be virtuous."

DR. STRAIGHT Your patience shall be rewarded. I'll come to the point at once. This compound known as Straightaline is the greatest hair tonic on earth. What will Straightaline do? Why, it cures dandruff, tetter itch, and all scalp diseases at once and forever. It makes hair grow on bald-headed babies. It makes curly hair straight as a stick in from one to ten days. Straightaline straightens kinky hair in from ten to thirty days and most wonderful of all, Straightaline straightens knappy or knotty hair.

(He hesitates.)

VOICE   Well?

DR. STRAIGHT   In three days.

VOICE   I'll take a bottle of dat.

DR. STRAIGHT   Wait, wait, wait, this is not all. I have another preparation, Oblicuticus, "Obl"—in this case, being an abbreviation of the word "obliterate." "Cuti"—taken from the word "cuticle," the outer skin—and "cuss" is what everybody does when the desired results are not obtained, but there is no such word as "fail." This wonderful face bleach removes the outer skin and leaves in its place a peachlike complexion that can't be duplicated—even by peaches. Changing black to white and vice versa. I am going to spend only one day in your city, but I am going to convince you by exhibiting a living evidence of my assertions that these two grand preparations, *Straightaline* and *Oblicuticus,* are the most wonderful discovery of modern times. *(Attendant stands up—he is possibly made up to be half white and half black.)* This young man is a martyr to science. Here you have the work of nature. Here the work of art. Here is the kinky hair here *(stage business with hair and skin color).* The long, silky straight hair, here the bronze of nature, here the peachlike complexion. Remember, I leave here tomorrow for Gatorville, Florida.

VOICES   Give me a bottle, give me a bottle.

DR. STRAIGHT   Wait a minute—I'm not here to sell, I'm only advertising these two grand articles, *Straightaline* and *Oblicuticus,* and after dispensing with a few coins of the realm, if you will accompany me to Skinners, I will place a few bottles of *Straightaline* and *Oblicuticus* at your disposal. Mind you, I'm not here to sell but to advertise. I'm not here to make money, but to give it away. *(He throws coins and exits. A quartet—the Barbers Society of Philosophical Research—enters and sings "Annie Laurie.")*

Strangely enough, the first night that he actually slept in the house on Seventh Avenue, he was sure that he was in Africa. He dreamt of natives with bare feet and painted faces who leapt wildly in frenzied dances. Of oppressive heat, and strange blood-curdling cries, of jabbering tongues and gatherings of crazed and perspiring people, all of whom seemed intent upon doing his person harm. This was his dream of Africa. There were no gentlemen in fine tailcoats, or wily businessmen, or property deals to be made. No kings, no queens, no princes, no aristocracy, just savages determined to punish him, and he abruptly opened his eyes and realized that he was covered in a heavy sweat. For a moment he had no idea of where he was, and he was unable to break clear of the terror of the dream. Mother was asleep, the moon spilling onto her face through a small gap in the floral drapes, but where was he? And then slowly his mind began to clear, and he heard traffic clipping by on the thoroughfare beneath the window. Seventh Avenue just above 135th Street. Harlem. As close to Africa as one can be in the United States of America, but his dreams were an embarrassment that he knew he must never admit to carrying in his head. He lay in bed in his home, his first real home outside his parents' house, and he understood that he was now a part of his wife's world. She, whose kisses tasted like cherries, had now taken control of a large part of his life, but he still possessed freedom in his work, and in his dreams, and although he felt affection for her he knew that Mother had already accepted that some things between this husband and wife would always remain a neatly executed step or two beyond her authority.

And then later, after the special gala performance of *In Dahomey*, and with the boisterous applause of the audience still buzzing in his head, and the syncopated frenzy of the orchestra still ringing in his ears, he sits alone in his dressing room and begins to remove the face. With each circular movement of the coarse towel more of the character falls away, revealing the true man underneath. He waits until he hears his fellow cast members tumble out of the theater in a state of high excitement and then he savors the silence. Soon heavy footsteps begin to echo along the corridor outside his dressing room, and there is a light knocking at his door. The stage manager enters without waiting for a reply, and he is surprised to find Bert still present and sitting all alone, naked without makeup. Bert observes a flicker of uncertainty register on the man's face, and he notices that the befuddled stage manager is suddenly unsure how to address the dignified star of the show. However, Mr. Williams makes it clear that there is no need for the man to say anything, for he raises a hand and smiles and lets him know that he will be leaving momentarily. After the stage manager departs, Bert continues to sit for a while, and then he stands and slowly opens the dressing room door. He edges his way past the props that line the narrow corridor before stepping out onto the noisy commotion of Forty-fifth Street. There is nobody by the stage door. His fellow players have not waited for him, but why would they? He feels sure that Mother would have reminded them that impromptu cast parties and such foolishness are not to Mr. Williams's liking, and so he begins the slow walk up Broadway, away from the lights, his feet hurting after the excesses of cakewalking, and shuffling around, and generally playing the fool with George. He walks slowly, with head erect and with an evenness of pace, through this most surprising of cities, which, even at this late hour, is still humming with traffic and noise and seemingly reluctant to either sleep or settle down. At the corner of Fifty-third Street he briefly stops and wonders whether he ought to at least show his face at Marshall's, but he understands that an appearance would probably bemuse, rather than please, his colleagues, and so he decides to walk four or five more blocks and then hail a ride and encourage the driver to trip through the park so that he might keep nature close by himself.

The corner of 135th and Seventh Avenue is his crossroads. The gentility of the neighborhood remains intact in the architecture, but the spirit of quiet contemplation that is suggested by the graceful curves and stately pillars is being slowly undermined by the energy of the new people. He pays the man, and overtips him a little, for it is late and he is always grateful to a driver who will come so far north when it is unlikely that he will be fortunate enough to find a fare to accompany him back south. He can see number 2309 with its short steep flight of steps leading up to the door. The narrow four-storey property is pinned between identical others, and is distinguishable only by the quality of the drapes that hang in the windows. This short row suggests something not quite grand, but something that is clearly beyond the ordinary, but he will not enter just yet, for his wife will still be at Marshall's, and he has yet to acquaint himself with the procedure of how to walk comfortably into an empty house. He stands and looks at number 2309, and then decides that rather than aimlessly wander the streets on his aching feet he will take a drink in Metheney's and have himself a little private contemplation. Mother will understand why her dispirited "Jonah Man" is reluctant to enter the house in its gloomy state, especially as he has just left a dark theater, and she will have no objections to his slipping inside Metheney's and making himself at home.

A silk-tongued George suggests to Ada that she looks tired and perhaps she ought to leave Marshall's and go home. Ada turns and smiles, and she announces to those in earshot that she has a headache and that it is probably time for her to leave, but she has a tight feeling in her chest that her colleagues suspect this to be untrue. Number 107 West 132nd Street is a handsome row house just off Sixth Avenue that is divided into apartments, with a tasteful flight of steps that lead to an elegant wooden door. Ada fishes carefully in her bag for her key, and even though she is far beyond people's eyes she tries to maintain a ladylike dignity. But her George has humiliated her again, although he always does so with the utmost charm. Before she left Marshall's he whispered to her that he had a chill and she should set a fire and warm up the apartment. He then informed her that when the drinking and carousing had died down a little he still had some business to conduct with Mr. Jesse Shipp and with the composers, Will Cook and Paul Dunbar, for there were a few numbers that needed touching up ahead of tomorrow night's show, and with rehearsal time being severely limited they would need to get their work started now. She had smiled at George, and having said good-bye to everybody she reassured her husband that she would have no trouble getting back by herself. "You take your time," were her final words. Lottie had begged Ada to let her accompany her on the journey back north, but Ada was a proud woman. She told Lottie to go back inside and enjoy herself. Everything would be fine. Once Ada found the key to the apartment, and opened the door and passed inside, she lit a fire and watched in silent fascination as the flames rose. She listened to the wood snapping and breaking loudly under the pressure of the heat. Then Ada looked up and peered out the window and into the empty street, and she caught herself reflected in the glass in this foolish repose and laughed out loud at her stupidity for she understood that once again she was unconsciously hoarding these slights like cards to be dealt on some future occasion, but she already understood that in order for her marriage to work she would have to ignore the pain of her husband's indiscretions and move on. Ada returned her gaze to the blazing fire, each flame describing a singular dance.

Bob Cole and Ernest Hogan stand by the bar and watch the *In Dahomey* company making their noise and swilling their drinks. Although the two colored veterans have not as yet seen the show, they *have* heard a good portion of what Cook and Dunbar have composed, for the two men tried out their new songs in Marshall's Lounge. As for the "business" part of the play, well everybody knows that these things are pretty much standard. A little verbal play, some spectacle, plenty of dance, a dash of disharmony, some vestige of tension, and that more or less covers everything. There have been Negro musical comedies before and so, the enviable Broadway location aside, what could be new? However, Cole and Hogan worry, for a success for one does not mean a success for all. The New York theatrical producers are notoriously fickle in their tastes, and they generally like to *pocket* just one colored man at a time, a man who they believe they can safely rely upon and promote, and George Walker is besporting himself as though he believes that he is that man, running his mouth off to Mr. Jesse Shipp and driving home his points with an erect forefinger. The small dark dandy from Kansas seems to have grown six inches as the evening has progressed, and Bob Cole and Ernest Hogan stand by the bar and order another drink without turning their heads to face the barman. They look straight ahead at the revelry, each man fully understanding what the other is thinking.

Leaving the Rockies behind at dawn, and setting out now across the vast expanse of the plains. He looks at the sun rising in the east and wonders if he should try to find some sleep. All night he has sat bolt upright and awake while his wife has slept peacefully on the noisy train, but his attention is now seized by the dazzling morning display of golden sunlight beginning to flood the prairie, while far off on the horizon there is a sudden flash of color, like a bird turning wing. It seems a whole lifetime ago that he left Florida and cut a swath across this continent from east to west on a ship with his wife and eleven-year-old son. Now here he is charging back across a land that is wild with large animals and dangerous men, but he feels safe on this train, watching the shifting landscapes of the huge country unfold before his eyes. How different from the small, economically impoverished island that he once called home. Riverside, California, has provided him with a roof and the possibility of making a decent living, but now he is reluctantly quarrying his way to the east coast to see the son that he has not seen in nearly ten years. His wife keeps their boy's few letters safely tucked away in a heavy book, and she often consults the yellowing sheets, running her finger along the words as she reads and rereads, trying to memorize the sentences as though they are the comforting words to a vaguely familiar song. However, it disappoints them both that as yet their secretive son has failed to send them an up-to-date portrait of either himself or his bride, their daughter-in-law, and they both worry that the gap that has grown up between them during this past decade may yet prove to be as wide and unbridgeable as the country that they are now traveling across.

I'M A JONAH MAN

(Lyrics and Music by Alex. Rogers)

My hard luck started when I was born, leas' so the old folks say.
Dat same hard luck been my bes' fren' up to dis very day.
When I was young my mamma's fren's to find a name they tried.
They named me after Papa and the same day Papa died.
For I'm a Jonah,
I'm an unlucky man.

My family for many years would look on me and then shed tears.
Why am I dis Jonah I sho' can't understand,
But I'm a good substantial full-fledged real first-class Jonah man.
A fren' of mine gave me a six-month meal ticket one day.
He said, "It won't do me no good, I've got to go away."
I thanked him as my heart wid joy and gratitude did bound.
But when I reach'd the restaurant the place had just burn'd down.
For I'm a Jonah,
I'm an unlucky man.

It sounds just like that old, old tale,
But sometimes I feel like a whale.
Why am I dis Jonah I sho' can't understand,
But I'm a good substantial full-fledged real first-class Jonah man.
My brother once walk'd down the street and fell into a coal hole.
He sued the man that owned the place and got ten thousand cold.
I figured this was easy so I jump'd in the same coal hole.
Broke both my legs and the judge gave me one year for stealin'
  coal.

Dancing in the Dark

For I'm a Jonah,
I'm an unlucky man.

If it rain'd down soup from morn till dark,
Instead of a spoon I'd have a fork.
Why am I dis Jonah I sho' can't understand,
But I'm a good substantial full-fledged real first-class Jonah man.

At the darkest point of the night he wakes suddenly with a dry throat and a vague tapping in his head. A shaft of moonlight stripes the bed and for a moment he studies the interplay of light and shadow before deciding what to do. He knows that it will take him some time before he becomes accustomed to living uptown, above the park in Harlem, but he understands that the woman next to him has made the right decision. Slowly he peels back the sheet and eases himself out of the bed and down onto the bare floorboards. The new carpet has yet to arrive. He stretches and then pushes his aching feet into a pair of slippers that have been deliberately placed beside the bed for this very purpose. Once he reaches the kitchen he nimbly swallows the first glass of water, then he takes his time with the second. He leaves the kitchen and wanders into the drawing room and sits on the sofa. From here he can look out at Seventh Avenue and relish the solitude of a windy night whose peace is broken only by the odd carriage that clips by, or a passing stranger hurrying his way home after an illicit assignation. He draws his feet up and lies back, glass still in hand, and then he reaches over and gingerly places the glass down on the floor beside him. It is light when he opens his eyes, and daylight is streaming through the window and laying a dappled map on the floor. Somebody has placed a blanket over him.

. . .

She stands over him and clutches the blanket to her chest. She has never really spoken to her sleeping husband about Florence, but she has expressed regret that her three nieces are growing up with neither a mother nor a father, their only relative being an aunt who they don't know. And he has listened to her, and encouraged her to bring the girls from East St. Louis to New York City, where they might have something akin to family life, but she knows that despite his protestations this is not what her husband really desires, for family life would be a distraction from his work. She carefully places the blanket over him and then she turns and leaves the drawing room. She had long ago convinced herself that to be touched was not that important, and she had imagined, as was the case with Mr. Sam Thompson, that once they were married he would choose not to press any serious claim upon her body. And being a gentleman, Mr. Williams has chosen not to do so.

He sits in nigger heaven and looks down at his West Indian son. At first he does not recognize him, and then, when he does, his stomach moves. This bewildered creature with a kinky wig, long ill-fitting white gloves, a shabby dress suit, oversized shoes, a battered top hat, sleeves and trousers that are too short, a mouth exaggerated by paint, this real funny nigger is his son? This coon with big eyeball-poppin' eyes is his child? He now understands why the boy has suggested that his wife stay at home and recuperate from the seemingly endless train journey. What has happened to his Bert? His Bahamian son who would sit patiently with him for hours and *study* the manner in which chickens threw dust behind them with their webbed feet. Father and son were inseparable. And then he brought the boy to Florida, and then on to California, in the hope that his child might achieve an education in the powerful country to the north. But this is not his son. This

Shylock. This grotesque simpleton shuffling about the stage who seems to be forever trapped in foolish predicaments. This buffoon. This nigger.

RAREBACK What in the world did you ask all those questions for?

SHYLOCK What's the use of being a detective if you can't ask questions even if you do know it won't do no good?

RAREBACK Well, Sherry, we'll have to keep our bluff anyway, so we'll go down to Gatorville, Florida, make old man Lightfoot think we are looking for the box he lost, and if we're lucky, we may get a chance to get to Dahomey with this emigration society.

SHYLOCK Say, man, have you got any idea how fast you'se carrying me through life? Ten minutes ago I was a soldier in the Salvation Army. Five minutes after that I'm a detective, and now you want me to be an emigrant.

RAREBACK (*laughing*) Stick to me and after we're in Dahomey six months, if you like it, I'll buy it for you. I'll tell the king over there that I'm a surveyor, and you're a contractor. If he asks for a recommendation, I'll tell him to go over to New York City and take a look at Broadway—it's the best job the firm ever did, and if he don't mind, we'll build him a Broadway in the jungle.

At the curtain call, with applause thundering in his ears, Bert looks straight out at the orchestra stalls and bows deeply. He gracefully receives the noisy evidence of their approval. However, as he straightens up at the waist he realizes that his heart is heavy with shame, and try as he might he cannot bring himself to look up and acknowledge his father. Upstairs in nigger heaven.

Act Two

(1903–1911)

He remembers the tall eleven-year-old boy whose father insisted that he still wear short pants, and who stared at the swath of foam that the ship was cutting into the tranquil waters of the Pacific Ocean as it edged a slow passage along the far coast of this new country. Above him the wind charged between the clouds, creating space for the lines of migrating birds who were returning north to where it was still cold and where snow clung stubbornly to the trees. The birds would soon realize their mistake. Back then young Bert discovered that he had no fondness for ocean voyages, and all these years later he remains uncomfortable when presented with only a watery horizon. These days he spends the greater part of his time downstairs in his cabin reading his well-thumbed copy of John Ogilby's *Africa,* and his wife is content to sit with him and minister to his needs. Elsewhere on the ship, the members of the Williams and Walker organization seem to be raucously enjoying themselves for he can occasionally hear their revelry, but he prefers some measure of detachment.

His wife has assured him that his company will not interpret his absence as a sign of either distance or aloofness, and that they will understand that he needs to rest, and so, during this saltwater crossing to England, he has seldom ventured out on deck. Handsome meals of various meats and vegetables are brought to his cabin on a silver tray, and sometimes, when the moon is bright and the ocean is unruffled, he and Mother will saunter upstairs, and cautiously slipping her arm through his, Mother will anchor herself to her husband and together they will promenade on deck. The white passengers know exactly who he is and they nod as the colored couple stroll by. After all, he is a man who is leading his own theatrical company—a man who has performed fifty-three times on Broadway.

Later, when alone in his cabin with his slumbering wife, he listens to the intoxicating rhythm of the sea. His toes stir for there is music in the light babbling of the swell as it laps against the hull of the vessel. He and his fifty so-called elite of coon performers have set out on a novel voyage for England, where Williams and Walker will present *In Dahomey* in the West End of London, and then tour the country with the production. Williams and Walker are doing well, and Bert has moved his parents into their own place and done everything he can to ensure that they feel settled in New York City, and he has made it clear to them that they must stay for as long as they wish. Relations between himself and his father remain somewhat strained, but neither one of them has found a way to address the troubling issue of the son's choice of career. Embarrassment hovers, like an unwelcome visitor, between the pair of them, but nevertheless the son has bought his father a barbershop business on Seventh Avenue, only a few doors from his own home, and to begin with he would occasionally wander by the parlor for a trim and shave. Having taken up a seat in the waiting area he would look proudly at his father's hands as they skillfully controlled both scissors and razor, and then it would be his turn to ease his way into the big leather armchair and sit quietly as his father pumped the metal lever with his foot and adjusted the seat downward. Having done so, the older man would tip the chair back, only slightly, but just enough so that the son felt helpless, and then he would produce his special pearl-handled razor. For a second the son's eyes might meet those of the father and the doubt would return. Although neither of them had ever acknowledged the source of the discontent that now existed between them, the son understood that it was probably he who should broach the uncomfortable subject, but by the time he was ready to do so it was generally too late, for his pop's slick hands would already be at work around the chin and neck, and the nature of the procedure meant that conversation was now impossible. However, whatever frustration his father was suffering from seemed to be safely locked away inside of him, and if silence was the price to be paid for the existence of a perplexing, but loving, peace between them, then the son was prepared to endure silence. Bert looks at his wife, who despite the gentle movement of the ship continues to sleep tranquilly with a hat fastened tightly to her head. He lights a cigarette and reopens his Ogilby, but he notices that his toes continue to dance to the music of the sea and it disappoints him that he appears to be helpless to arrest the nigger in him.

The dressing room is the one place where he is able to think clearly, for the silence and privacy suggest to him the sanctity of a church. The dressing room is a place where he can sit alone and remember all that has gone before, and imagine all that is still to unfold. The mirror is the most important part of the room. The mirror and the lightbulbs. Plenty of bright, gleaming lightbulbs arranged tastefully around the perimeter of the mirror glass. And a door with a good lock to it. Two chairs, please. One in front of the mirror, and a softer chair where a man might relax and read a newspaper or a book and enjoy some peaceful contemplation. These few items are all a man needs in his dressing room. At the New York Theatre, at Forty-fifth Street and Broadway, where they played *In Dahomey*, he enjoyed a perfectly adequate dressing room. Whenever he needed privacy he simply locked the door and withdrew from everybody. A major New York critic had penned a favorable notice of the show, but the man described the star as an amiable coon who possessed "magnificent white grinders in a cavernous mouth." Every evening, having washed his face and applied the towel, a despondent Bert stared into the mirror but he failed to see the amiable coon with the cavernous mouth who the influential critic had described.

George enjoys decorating his dressing room with large and somewhat vulgar bouquets of sweet-smelling flowers, but Bert does not care for this kind of ostentation and so he seldom visits with George. In fact, Bert does not care for lace cloths, or perfumed water, or soft plump cushions, and there are always far too many people in George's dressing room, but George understands his partner's difficulties with strangers. When George wishes to talk with Bert he frequently travels to his colleague's dressing room with a liquor bottle in one hand, and he is always careful to lock the door behind him before he sits down. He understands that if they are to talk, it is he who must visit Bert's quarters, and so slender George, with his perfectly oval face and clothes that would grace a prince, grins at Bert and places his insubstantial weight on a creaky wooden chair and then lights his cigar and pours them both a drink as he makes ready to engage his partner.

.   .   .

"Bert, you really want to take the show to London?" George pulls eagerly on his cigar. "I thought you didn't care for sailing on water. Man, I thought you just wanted to stay here and work on another show."

Bert picks up George's bottle and pours them both a second shot of whiskey. They clink glasses.

"If the Englishman wants to see *In Dahomey*, then maybe we should show the Englishman what we got."

"So what you think we got, then?"

Bert laughs now—slow, rumbling laughter that rocks the room. George's eyes light up.

"Come on, man, what you think we got that the Englishman needs to see? Besides high-toned women, fine music, fresh comedy, and all the dance stepping in the world?"

"Well," says Bert, as he swirls the whiskey in his glass, "I figure that's plenty to be going on with, don't you? I'm ready to ease on over there and show the Englishman what we got."

"You ready to cross water to do so?"

"Ain't no other way of getting there."

"Maybe the English will treat us with a little more respect."

Bert continues to laugh. "George, you think they could treat us with less?"

Bert remembers his short week in New York vaudeville just before the opening of *In Dahomey*. He remembers sharing the bill with Maurice Barrymore, who, having finished his own act, liked to stand in the wings at every performance and peruse Bert's technique, but this scrutinizing never troubled Bert. Everybody took from everybody else, and he saw no reason why this man should be any different. However, Barrymore's studiousness annoyed the stagehands for Barrymore was not supposed to admire a man like Bert. Over the years, Bert has endured many problems with ill-bred stagehands, but nothing to match the difficulties that he encountered during this short week. A particularly rough-hewn man asked Barrymore if he really liked the nigger coon, but Barrymore simply glared. As Bert came offstage, and passed by them both, he heard the boorish stagehand say, "Yeah, he's a good nigger, he knows his place." Without breaking his stride, or looking at either man, Bert replied, "Yes, a good nigger knows his place. Going there now. Dressing room one." Barrymore punched the stagehand in his mouth. Later, when George heard about the incident, he was livid, but Bert would not talk with George, or with anyone, about the unsettling episode.

Well, Bert, if the choices we got is working on another show, going back to vaudeville, or going to England, then let's go to England. Another show can wait a while, but I don't got your stomach, Bert, so I sure as hell won't be doing no more vaudeville, no sir, not me. I reckon that George Walker is better than working with iron jaw acts, and regurgitators and acrobats straight from the ships, and long-limbed girls from burlesque who don't understand that there's no place in vaudeville for bare legs and foul language. America got those Wright boys up in the air, and automobiles rolling down the streets, and some kind of baseball World Series, and this is a new country for everybody, including the colored man. Damn it, we've gone beyond getting up there three or four times a day, even if they do give us prime billing. Everything in goddamn vaudeville is always rush, rush, rush, with the Jews playing the Germans, and the Germans playing the Irish, and the Irish playing the Chinese, and everybody thinking they can play colored because what's a poor colored man going to do to stop them? We coloreds got to be doing more respectable work like *In Dahomey* instead of playing damn-fool happy creatures who between steamboat arrivals just pick cotton or fry fish until it's time to slouch off again and tote some cargo and sing

some coon songs. Williams and Walker done gone beyond vaudeville. We got to take our time and do what we do with style. *In
Dahomey* is the thing, Bert, and no reason for us to be rushing to
produce another show, or for you to be going back to no foolish
vaudeville. We should do like you say and take our colored tails
across that water to old London and show them what we got.

Bert always takes dressing room number one, while George
establishes himself in dressing room number two. This is the way
that it is, and neither man has ever discussed the subject, and if
George has any cause for complaint, then Bert has not heard anything about it. George refills their glasses with whiskey and Bert
proposes that they drink a toast. To England, and to their forth-
coming salty voyage, during which, each evening, they will temporarily lose the sun on the other side of the sea.

On the long passage across the Atlantic Ocean, Bert's cabin is his
dressing room. It is his place of refuge, but in his cabin there are
no oversized shoes, no ill-fitting pants, no overventilated coat.
There is no smell of burnt cork, no communion with anxiety, no
sense of performance hanging in the air. He has to neither apply
nor does he have to scrape off the black from his face. He does
not have to peer cautiously into the mirror wondering if any signs
of disfigurement remain. His lips, are they normal? In *this* dressing room he need not look at himself with the sadness that pre-
cedes and concludes a performance. Here on the SS *Aurania*, his
superior cabin is a dressing room where disguise is unnecessary.
In the corner a silent clock stands tall, its wooden casing polished
by the touch of many hands. He is leaving America behind.

His company trusts him. This evening he sits at a table with his
wife and looks across at the fifty colored men and women huddled together in one corner of the ship's dining room. They are

sailing with him to England, following him over the horizon to a Europe that most of them have never seen. They are excited, and George is both entertaining them and lecturing them. Occasionally George looks up and glances in Bert's direction and their eyes meet. There is a little nod of the head from both of them. The white diners look on in bemusement, but they stare hard at Bert, disturbed by the fact that his dignified presence among them is beginning to challenge their sense of who he is. Coon. The novelty is becoming tedious. Without his disguise their ability to trust him is being seriously undermined, and if truth be told, they would rather he knew his place and joined the Negro rabble.

I make my entrance with only a small spotlight penetrating the darkness. I thrust my white-gloved hands through the curtains and into the light. Before they see me they see my gloved hands twisting and turning, and then they make out the rest of me as I carefully edge my way between the heavy velvet drapes and stand still and slowly look all around. They do not know what to do. It is only when I move that the problems begin. I shuffle and they laugh. I show them that I am clumsy and they laugh. I stand still and they do not know what to do. Until I move I might be pitiable. It is only when I move that they recognize me. I enjoy the beginning, with my white gloved hands, and the small spotlight, and edging my way through the curtains and standing still. But they require both the cork and the movement, the broad nigger smile and the shuffle, and only then do they know me. Only then am I welcome in their house.

The white cliffs of Dover are white. It is morning and the whole company is on deck, their necks rolled in scarves, their hands holding collars tight, staring at England rising up through the mist. The first light of dawn is igniting the sea, and somewhere in the distance the forlorn howling of foghorns drifts through the gloom. Above their heads a thin line of gulls dip on the early morning breeze and then bank steeply away from the ship in the direction of the open sea. Lottie holds her husband's arm and gently tugs him closer to her. The midwest suddenly seems a long way distant, but she realizes with both surprise and pride that her new husband has traveled even farther than she has. If only Flo could see her now; in Europe with her husband's company, standing near the prow of the SS *Aurania*, bringing colored America to England. America's Shylock Homestead looks down at her, a thin smile creasing his lips, and she recognizes loneliness behind his sad eyes and wishes more than anything in the world that there was some way for her to bring sunshine into his life. She looks up at him and smiles and then a sudden gust of wind threatens to dislodge her hat and she quickly reaches up a hand and clamps it down on her head. Might England be a new beginning for them both? She asks the question, but only with her eyes.

He walks alone in Hyde Park, where he observes the persistent wind blowing furiously at the dresses of young women, and where he tips his hat to passersby, who in turn are keen to tip their hats to the colored stranger. At all times of the day and night a fog seems to hang over the city like a giant cloud that is reluctant to disperse. A plump-lipped but otherwise slack-faced woman, with an off-white egg of a face, tries to engage him in conversation. He can see that the woman dresses well, but it soon strikes him that her expensive tastes merely mask the fact that she is one who walks the streets for profit and he promptly hurries on his way. He detects a problem in this sad city, under its thick blanket of despair, and he chooses a park bench by a pond and sits in order to better examine these people. He notices that despite the cold this pond is not capped with ice, and then he turns his attention to the faceless people, their heads hanging low, a seemingly endless caravan of misery. They trudge with shoulders hunched and with furled umbrellas in tightly clenched hands, and then he realizes that even the spring flowers that surround him appear to be pouting. Where is the joy in this country, or among these people? Where is the energy? Already he is wary of how Williams and Walker will be received once *In Dahomey* opens. He wants to feel comfortable in this new country, but the beat is wrong. Something is out of tune in England, and he knows that his company, huddled away in their cramped rooms at the damp hotel, they feel it too.

He sits in his Shaftsbury Avenue dressing room and he stares into the mirror. The booking agent has urged him to understand that the English audiences will expect a certain type of Negro authenticity, but what the man does not know is that a determined George has made sure that their own performers can never stoop to deliver such crude "authenticity." The booking agent has led Bert to believe that the patrons of the English theater are probably waiting for their American visitors to take to the stage and entertain them with a volley of raggy coon songs, while all the time winding their tan behinds at them like flags. If this is the case, then in all likelihood Williams and Walker will probably disappoint their hosts, but it is too late now, for the impatient English stage manager is already stalking the corridors. ("Come along, my sons. Chop-chop.") The man bellows in his thick cockney tongue, demanding that the Yank darkies make their way to the wings, and as he does so Bert's colored heart begins to pound.

The audience loves the dancing. A bold couple even takes to the aisle and imitates the Negro performers, who in turn stop and applaud their English impersonators. Ada refuses to applaud for she considers the audience disrespectful, and once they are all safely offstage she loudly conveys her dismay to George, who promises to discuss the situation with Bert. However, her husband is undisturbed by this English mimicry, for his primary concern is that they should attract a paying audience and therefore make their stay in this miserable country a short but profitable one. Once Ada has passed into the women's dressing room, George stands backstage by himself and resolves to say nothing to Bert. The following evening another limey couple takes to the aisle and again a furious Ada refuses to applaud them.

The English critics are puzzled by *In Dahomey*, and in particular, they fail to understand why the vast majority of the colored girls are light-skinned with straightened hair. George gives a newspaper interview in which he explains at length about the popularity of hair-straightening products and skin-bleaching creams among colored women, but to a man the English critics seem disappointed by the very few specimens of genuine sable beauty upon their stage. Especially so, notes one apoplectic scribe, given the fact that the back-to-Africa theme appears to be so much in vogue among Negroes, and this subject matter, which falls squarely within the current theatrical craze of locating Americans in queer lands, would seem to demand some genuine exoticism. Are we to assume, he thunders, that these near-white creatures in highly unlikely complex costumes, and displaying exquisite and alluring mannerisms, are the type of creatures that we would find were we to journey to that dismal continent? This one man lambastes the whole enterprise as "preposterous," but his voice is not in the majority. Each evening a respectable audience flows up Shaftsbury Avenue from Piccadilly Circus to witness the Negro players and enjoy the spectacle of them performing their newly fashionable dance, the cakewalk; and then, a few weeks into their engagement, they receive the honor of a royal visit, which serves only to confirm the newfound English celebrity of Messrs. Williams and Walker. A week after the highly successful royal visit, the whole company receives the ultimate accolade of a *command* to perform privately in the garden of the king's residence, Buckingham Palace.

> In size as well as ability is Mr. Bert Williams a big comedian, and in the vicinity of Shaftsbury Avenue, where he is frequently to be seen striding his way lurchingly to and from the theatre, with his great head turning curiously and solemnly first one side and then another, like an elephant on the broad path ("Bun Avenue") at the Zoo, he is already known as "Big Black Bert." The delightful thing about his impersonation of Shylock Homestead is that the actor, not withstanding that it is to him chiefly the audience looks for amusement, is never seen forcing the fun or pushing himself forward in the least. With his heavy, rocking gait, he "hovers around" like one who has found himself on the stage by taking the wrong passage, and thinks he may as well stay there since no one has interfered with him.

> *MOSTLY ABOUT PEOPLE*, LONDON, 1903

And then they tour England. Dark-skinned missionaries in the heartland of Britain moving diligently between Hull, Peckham, Newcastle, Sheffield, and Manchester. Bert especially enjoys Oxford, the center of books and learning, and once they leave this ancient city the company travels north and eventually crosses the invisible border into Scotland, where they offer *In Dahomey* to a new race of people. In Edinburgh, the capital of this new kingdom, Bert is taken in by a secret group of men who wish to honor him. He becomes a mason, a colored man in Waverly Lodge No. 597 of Edinburgh, Scotland, and by degrees he enters further into a foreign world of respectable connections. It transpires that it is his offstage clerical dignity that has also impressed these fellows, for they recognize in Bert the type of man in whose shadow people might seek shade and protection. But this is not to say that they don't appreciate his darky antics. He has made them all laugh with his droll singing and his loose-limbed dancing, but the shrewd Scots suspect that behind Mr. Williams's broad grinning mouth something mournful is stirring for their new American brother performs as though he derives little joy from his tomfoolery.

When the assembled Scottish pressmen ask an exasperated George to demonstrate the cakewalk to them, he smiles weakly then climbs to his aching feet, noisily pushes back a few chairs, and begins with a sporty strut.

> Bow to the right
> Bow to the left
> Then you take your place
> Be sure to have a smile on your face
> Step high with lots of style and grace
> With a salty prance
> Do a ragtime dance
> Step way back and get your gun
> With a bow look wise
> Make goo-goo eyes
> For that's how the cakewalk's done.

George cocks an eyebrow to make himself appear more rakish, but he can no longer maintain the pretense. This buttery exchange, lubricated with flattery on both sides, is turning his stomach. Williams and Walker have made their coin and he is now eager that they should return home as hastily as possible.

As the ship moves slowly in the direction of the United States, Bert stands on deck with his partner. He turns to George, and silently revisits the same questions that have plagued him through many lonely evenings in the foggy country that they are now leaving behind. Is the colored performer to be forever condemned to pleasing a white audience with farce, and then attempting to conquer these same people with music and dance? Is the colored American performer to be nothing more than an exuberant, childish fool named Aunt Jemima, Uncle Rufus, or simply Plantation Darky, who must be neither unique nor individual? Can the colored American ever be free to entertain beyond the evidence of his dark skin? Can the colored man be himself in twentieth-century America? He remembers long nights drinking good whiskey and worrying about these matters in Jimmie Marshall's hotel with his partner, and Bob Cole and Ernest Hogan, and he recalls an increasingly petulant George talking loudly about his determination to kill the chicken-stealing, crap-shooting, razor-toting, gin-guzzling, no-good nigger in white people's heads. Bert stands on deck and continues to look at his partner, but sadly he understands what George thinks about him. His comic timing, his wide range of facial expressions, his much-admired technical skills—he knows that his partner respects these well-honed talents, but he also knows that his partner longs to say, "Bert, you look and act like a nigger and we colored Americans no longer recognize you for we are trying to move on." But George says nothing, and George has never said anything directly, and Bert turns away from his friend and narrows his eyes as the sea breeze begins to gather strength. In the distance he can see faintly visible steamers trailing dissolving smoke as they hug the line of the horizon and inch slowly in the direction of America. Bert pulls a pack of cigarettes from the inside pocket of his jacket, and then he cups his hand and strikes a match, which immediately sputters out. He understands how George feels about his blackface performance, but until his partner finds words that neither admonish nor accuse, then an uneasy discord will exist between them. Bert finally lights his cigarette and then he tosses the match overboard. He stares plaintively at the sea, but he feels the weight of George's critical eyes and understands that his carefully calibrated blackface act is now beginning to corrode their partnership.

It was in Scotland that Bert was finally able to discover more about this elusive man Ogilby, whose book he loved to study. He learned that John Ogilby was born outside of Dundee in 1600, the son of a well-heeled Scottish gentleman. He published his *Africa* in 1670, a volume that—Bert had always felt convinced—should he study it sufficiently, would eventually provide him with the evidence that every Pullman porter was descended from a king. It was this leather-bound tome that he utilized for proof that Africa was a continent of history and tradition, and not one of rude chaos; and the act of entering this book always enabled Bert to experience the temporary peace of being able to moor himself in some other place.

AFRICA: / BEING AN / ACCURATE DESCRIP-TION / OF THE / REGIONS / OF / Egypt, Barbary, Lybia, and Billedulgerid, / The LAND of / Negroes, Guinee, AEthiopia, and the Abyssines, / With all the Adjacent Islands, either in the Mediterranean, / Atlantick, Southern, or Oriental Sea, belonging there-

unto. / With the several Denominations of their / Coasts,
Harbors, Creeks, Rivers, Lakes, Cities, / Towns, Castles,
and Villages. / THEIR / Customs, Modes, and Manners,
Languages, / Religions and Inexhaustible Treasure; /
With their / Governments and Policy, variety of Trade
and Barter, / And also of their / Wonderful Plants,
Beasts, Birds, and Serpents. / _____ / Collected and
Translated from most <u>Authentick Authors</u>, / And
Augmented with later Observations; / Illustrated with
Notes, and Adorn'd with peculiar Maps, and proper
Sculptures, / By <u>JOHN OGILBY</u> Esq; / Master of His
Majesties <u>REVELS</u> in the Kingdom of <u>IRELAND.</u> /
_____ / <u>LONDON</u>, / Printed by <u>Tho. Johnson</u> for the
Author, and are to be had at his / House in <u>White Fryers</u>,
M.DC.LXX.

I'D LIKE TO BE A REAL LADY

Introduced by Ada Overton Walker in Williams
and Walker's latest production, In Dahomey

Ada walks with him on deck and again she asks him about Eva,
although she never mentions the woman by name. His wife is
angry and distressed, and sometimes her behavior frightens him.
George stares out toward the distant point where the rough mat-
ing of sea and sky fuses at the horizon, and he carefully prepares
yet another story as a substitute for the truth for he cannot tell his
wife that in his soul he is sailing back across the broad expanse of
the Atlantic Ocean toward Eva, who, one night after the show,
approached him in his high-scented dressing room at the New
York Theatre. A half hour later, Eva unlocked the door and

stepped back out into the corridor knowing full well what the rest of the company were thinking. Eva does not care, and George likes this about her, but Ada *does* care, for this is not just another of her husband's anonymous women, this is Eva Tanguay, and Ada believes that her full-lipped, ebony-hued husband has no place with a flame-haired, hip-swinging white maiden. Ada cares, and at least to begin with she said nothing, but when she eventually asked her husband to deny the rumors he lied to her face, and she knew that he was lying. And now again, on this ship, Ada asks him about Eva Tanguay and George notices that his wife has a crazy glint in her coal black eyes and so he kisses her delicately on the cheek and then ushers her from the deck of the ship and in the direction of their cabin, where he will gently cradle her small breasts as though they were newborn twins for he knows that his Ada is partial to such attention.

I'd like to be a real lady, yes,
I'd like to be the genuine,
I'd like to look a real mansion in the face
and say to my friends "that's mine,"
I'd like a blue grass lawn on which to give my pink green tea,
I'd like an English butler to announce my company,
I'd like a golden sleeping room
a maid to bathe me in perfume,
I'd like to be a real lady.

—You needing to talk?
Bert leans against the railing as he asks the question. Theirs has been the most successful tour of Britain by any American company, white or colored, but melancholy sits heavily on both men's shoulders. George looks up at his friend and pauses a moment before replying.
—Got plenty on my mind. How about you?

Bert pulls on his cigarette and stares out at the gently undulating blanket of black water. For days now they have been making their painfully slow way back in the direction of New York City, and they have decided that once they return home they will take *In Dahomey* on the road in the United States. Bert pulls on his cigarette and chortles to himself. He turns to face George.

—I guess we've both been away for a good long while.

—I don't know if I'm ready to go back yet.

—You ready to become an Englishman, George?

Bert laughs at his own joke, and a small smile appears at the edge of his partner's mouth. George turns from him and looks up at the clouds racing across the darkening sky, and Bert flicks his dying stub over the edge and watches it land on the water, where it bobs furiously in the eddy before being swallowed up. Bert removes a crumpled pack from his inside jacket pocket, cups his hand, and lights another cigarette. He has spoken again with his wife about her giving up the stage and focusing on their new home and her husband's career, and she seems to be slowly acclimatizing to the idea. In fact, she confessed that her first husband had wanted her to abandon what he called "hoofing and prancing" and she resisted, but these days she appreciates that she is older and less spry and her ambitions are now primarily invested in developing a shared life with her new husband. She reached out and touched her husband's arm as she said this, and Bert rewarded her with a smile. However, out here on deck, he senses that his wife probably still requires a little time by herself for the idea of retirement to take a proper hold, and so he decides to lean against the railing in the stiff breeze and keep company with George. There is no pressure on either of them to speak.

He asks Eva where she is from. "Canada, honey, then Massachusetts. I'm like a big storm blowing south to sweep your stylish little colored behind off its seat." She laughs and then begins to unbutton her blouse. "Girl's gotta do what a girl's gotta do if she's gonna get on in this world." Eva stops and stares at him. "Mr. Walker, don't you intend to step out of those clothes?" George leans forward and begins to unbuckle his shoes. "George, baby, you ever see my costume of dollar bills and shiny pennies?" George shakes his head. He stands and slips out of his jacket, which he hangs neatly on the back of his dressing room chair. "But I heard about it. Heard it scared every man in town, and excited a few of them too." Eva's hoarse laugh rattles noisily around her throat. "Well, that's the idea, George. That's the idea, honey." Eva puts a shapely leg up on a chair and begins to roll her stocking carefully down toward her ankle. She looks at George as she does so. "Now then, honey, when Eva takes hold of you you'd better keep your voice down unless you want everybody in the theater to hear you hollering for mercy." George fumbles quickly at his belt, and then he pulls the tail of his shirt out of his pants with a lively clean jerk. Eva places the now bare creamy leg back on the floor and hoists the other leg up and onto the chair. "And, honey, when I sing 'That's Why They Call Me Tabasco,' I mean just that. I'm a girl who can make a man feel good and hot all over, so you ready to have some fun?" George lets his pants drop to the floor. As he neatly steps clear of them it isn't just this one song that he is thinking of. Eva's celebrated repertoire includes "It's All Been Done Before but Not the Way I Do It," "I Want Someone to Go Wild with Me," and her famous "I Don't Care." Eva looks directly at George as he folds his pants properly and drapes them over the back of the chair. "George, I heard a lot of things about you, and about what you got down there in those pants of yours, but you really think you're ready for Eva Tanguay?" She sits on the wooden chair and opens her legs slightly. Eva watches as George removes his shirt and she notices the tight muscles that climb his stomach like a ladder. She reaches up and releases her breasts from the prison of her corselette, and she wets her lips with the end of her tongue. "Georgie, you know I don't think you got what it takes." Eva lets out a large raucous laugh and slaps her thigh. "Whatever it is you're hiding in those drawers don't look like it's gonna be of much use to old Eva."

—How's things between you and Lottie?

Bert doesn't turn to look at his friend. He continues to scan the horizon, which, as the last slither of light fades rapidly from the sky, and the moon and stars declare themselves, is becoming increasingly difficult to discern.

—Well, things with Mother and myself is pretty much how you expect things between a man and his wife to be.

—And how's that?

Bert abandons the horizon, and he looks directly at George and sees that his partner's eyes are bright and troubled. Bert sighs deeply, and then he decides that he will speak slowly, but from the heart.

—Well, my wife has certain expectations that I confess I don't feel any obligation to fulfill. Nothing personal, I just figure my focus is elsewhere, but that doesn't help her loneliness none. I expect that most of them are probably the same way. Needing to have you organized in a manner that makes them feel safe and appreciated, but that isn't always easy for a busy man with a career. Men like us got professional worries that have to be accommodated, but that don't always square with them, so it soon becomes a matter of each learning to live with the disappointment of the other. That's pretty much how things are between me and Mother. Each learning to live with the disappointment of the other.

George purses his lips and quietly nods.

—I hear you. The only problem is I don't think Ada's done much to disappoint me.

Fact is, I'm the one who's been doing all the disappointing and I guess it's just eating me up a little.

—You sweet on somebody in particular, George? Miss Tanguay?

George laughs.

—I never known you to get stuck on just one.

—Hell, I never known me to get stuck on just one either. It ain't exactly what I was expecting, you know. You'd think that all this time away in England, and a few new adventures, would wash her right out from under my skin. But she got something, Bert, and I don't know what it is.

—You sure you don't know what it is?

—Hell, that flash is just for show. But beyond all that foolishness, there's a real bighearted woman there.

Bert stares at his friend, but he deems it best to say nothing further. George likes to live dangerously, he knows this, but as stubborn as Ada can be, doesn't she at least have a right to some dignity? Bert continues to look pitifully at his friend and partner, who now peers out into the blackness of the night. When he has finished his cigarette Bert will leave George by himself and go back downstairs to Mother.

George stands alone on the deck of the ship and thinks of Eva. He knows all about her. In fact, how could he *not* know about her? Controversy follows Eva wherever she goes. Three times she has married, and each time she has chosen a second-rate show business personality. First there was a dancer named John W. Ford, then a vaudevillian named Roscoe Ails, and now she has taken up with a pianist named Alexander Brooke, but for Eva marriage is never a serious affair. She openly admits that her middle name should be "Trouble," for trouble always seems to find her, and when trouble slips out of sight she goes looking for it. If she is not being arrested for brawling on a train, or being discovered by detectives in a hotel room where she is having an affair with her press agent, she is complaining to the audience, as she did in Sharon, Pennsylvania, that she is displeased with the size of the mirror in her dressing room and rounding on them by calling them "small-town saps." In Louisville, Kentucky, she was successfully sued for $1,000 by a stagehand who she pushed down a flight of stairs, and a local court fined her a further $50. One evening in Evansville, Indiana, she overslept and missed a performance so the manager fined her $100, which prompted her to take a knife and slash the curtains of the theater to ribbons. This is George's girl. Eva Tanguay, who told him that when she finally tracked down her birth mother she got a letter in reply from the woman stating that she had absolutely no wish to meet her. Eva, who smokes while she is eating, and whose nails are often chipped and dirty, and who keeps a purse in the cleavage between her breasts. He stands alone on the deck of the ship and feels a shiver surge through his body as the night breeze begins to pick up strength. He is going back to America, but the truth is he is returning to Eva, even though he fears it's unlikely that she will still be waiting for him. He continually asks himself, Why this one? Of all the women with whom he has exchanged his colored fame for their favors, why this untamable one?

Back in Harlem, he sleeps now in a different room than Mother, but she never mentions this fact. These days, neither the thought nor the touch of his wife produces any stirring of ardor in his loins and so he eventually deemed it best to make a dignified, if somewhat clumsy, exit from their bedroom. Surrounded by his precious hardbound volumes, which sit on handsome dark oak shelves, their spines broken, the leather rubbed thin, he sits up late into the night and smokes cigarette after cigarette as he reads. In the morning the din of street traffic announcing a new day often finds him still seated but asleep, the book having slid to the floor at some point in the night. Bert's triumphant return to the United States and the pressures of his increased fame have finally convinced his wife that indeed she can now afford to retire from the stage and devote herself to home and husband. However, her disconsolate days, and lonely nights, begin to trouble her for she is incapable of fully inhabiting this new role of wife and lady of the house if her husband is reluctant to take up his part. The national tour of *In Dahomey* having been completed, each evening he now leaves with a curt but polite farewell for Hammerstein's Victoria, where he and George are playing a limited season. And then, after the show, he stops in at Metheney's before ambling back to 2309 Seventh Avenue under the cover of night. George, on the other hand, often hurries over to the Variety Theatre to catch the last part of Eva's act for he finds himself possessed by an intoxicating affection that he thought himself incapable of feeling for any woman. Although Ada is still slender, and firm-bodied, George understands that he is making a young widow of his wife, but what can he do?

> At the Victoria, Williams and Walker perform "The Detective Story" from their hit in the all-black musical *In Dahomey*. In the humorous sketch Walker tells stories about Nick Carter and the Old Sleuth. Williams sings his well-known songs "Nobody" and "Pretty Desdamone."

> HAMMERSTEIN'S VICTORIA PLAYBILL,
> NOVEMBER 1905

Having unleashed every fighting phrase at his disposal, George now glares at their promoter and tries to control his desire to spit in the face of this fool. Why can Bert not see that this man is talking down to them? And if he does see it, why can he not open his mouth and say something? After all, they are stars. Williams and Walker are no longer boys fleeing Cripple Creek, and this is not the Barbary Coast. They have headlined on Broadway and in London's West End, and it is to Broadway that they should be returning with their new show, *Abyssinia*, which, like their previous success, will eschew the razors, the chickens, the loose women, and the low talk of regular coon performances. They are the most important, and the most serious, colored performers in America so who is this man to suggest that they now play at Columbus Circle? George struggles manfully to control his temper, but Bert embraces silence and his partner looks helplessly at him. Sometimes Bert behaves as though his makeup is an extra layer of skin that he cannot rub away, and George worries that perhaps both Bert's unfortunate blackface performance *and* his disturbingly accommodating personality are becoming somewhat confused in his partner's mind. George Walker shakes his head for his disposition has now soured, trapped as he is between a damn fool promoter and a foolish friend, neither of whom seem to have noticed that they have entered the twentieth century.

Since their return from England, both Bert and George have been discovering something nearly akin to a new city. Long Acre Square was now proudly styling itself Times Square, while a novel subway system from City Hall, in the south, all the way north to 145th Street was enabling New Yorkers of all stations of life to ride either above or beneath the earth. Colored citizens and performers continued to flood uptown to Harlem, and although life at Marshall's wasn't what it used to be, Jimmie Marshall was still committed to working out the life of his lease. The pair of them greet a visibly deflated proprietor, and then sit quietly by themselves in the far corner of the lounge. It is clear to all who look on that there is no desire on the part of either man for social small talk, and so despite their fame nobody approaches them. George speaks first. "If we have to go to court, then we go to court. I keep telling you, ain't no way we can play at Columbus Circle, not after Broadway. It makes no damn sense." Bert slowly fingers his cigarette. He takes a long draw, then exhales, all the while looking directly at his partner, and George waits patiently until his friend is good and ready to speak. "You know," begins Bert, "if you don't mind making our business public for all the world to see, then I guess you must go right ahead. But I'd rather we did this another way. A quieter way." George leans back in his chair and sighs deeply, but he remains determined that there should be no dispute between the two of them. He watches as Bert jams his cigarette into the ashtray, the frustration of the action betraying his exterior calm. "Bert, if we gotta make public our drawers in order to get rid of this white fool, then that's what we must do." Bert watches his friend's indignation rise. "Man, we're just looking for a fair shake and we're not his boys, not then and not now." George pauses. "Especially not now." Bert looks at his partner and then slowly nods his head as he reaches for another cigarette.

George sits alone in the dark. The framed photograph on the mantelpiece of the living room seizes his attention, and he recalls the anxious white man who corralled together the four finely dressed colored entertainers for this promotional picture. The man barked instructions and tried to position the Negro dancers without actually touching any of them, but the more he worked with the chocolate dandies the clearer it became that all four of them were a trifle unsure of themselves. The man was used to people who were keen to strike poses that might satisfy him— snap quickly, one, two, then a third, head held high, hold it, a pose, recline the neck, drape the arm, that's it, that's it, good—but these colored dancers moved nervously around one another in his studio. The photograph continues to seize George's attention. Ada is out rehearsing, and for the first time in many months George finds himself alone in their apartment. Just what did this man see as he peered through his lens? What did he actually witness before he ushered them out of his studio and then dipped their faces into a shallow trough of acid?

George sits alone in the dark. Beyond this one photograph there are no images of him in their apartment. She does not keep any of him alone, nor does she treasure any of them together. This one photograph only. A beginning, but no story going forward. For the past three weeks Eva has not returned his messages. She was on the road out in the midwest, but he knows that she has now returned to New York City, yet she will not respond to his hand-delivered notes, nor will she take his calls. However, according to the gossipmongers, there are others who are keen to maintain company with sporting George Walker, who these days keeps the newspaper columnists busy with tales of his various enterprises. George stands and removes the photograph from the mantelpiece, and then he sits back on the sofa. Poor Ada will soon be home. A beginning, but no story going forward.

Although I was too young to have ever met him, I had heard plenty of talk about Mr. George Walker. Apparently he was everything his song "Bon Bon Buddy" suggested, with his high silk hat, fine leather gloves, polished monocle, and malacca cane. The photographs make it clear why he boasted that no white man could ever wear his clothes for there was indeed an exuberant quality to his wardrobe. His physique, although small, was magnificently poised, and Mr. Walker clearly carried himself with a nobility that one generally associates with the more physically striking of the colored prizefighters. It was rumored that his was the first tan box coat on Broadway, and although during our interview Mr. Williams was not able to confirm this tale, my own suspicion was that there was probably some substance to this rumor. His cakewalk was, of course, peerless, and although there were many pretenders, both white and colored, Mr. George Walker was universally recognized as the master of this particular dance.

When Ada returns home she discovers that George has already set forth on his evening adventures, and the framed photograph has been removed from the mantelpiece and is lying abandoned on the sofa. She takes off her coat and sits before the mirror and begins to comb out the kinks in her hair. Although he may betray her with a chorus line of impressionable girls, she has managed to convince herself that in every other way he remains faithful to her. But tonight this is no longer enough for Ada. She puts down the comb and picks up a pair of scissors. Having hurriedly removed the photograph from its ornate brass frame, she carefully slices the offending image into neat strips.

They sit together in silence and wait for the clerk of the court to summon them back into the dimly lit courtroom so they can hear the verdict of the judge. Bert knows that he was right, for the business accounts of Williams and Walker have been made uncomfortably public. The deposition from their lawyer revealed that the American tour of *In Dahomey*, which followed hard on the heels of their success in England, turned out to be extremely profitable. Everywhere the cash register announced success, and these days they each earn upward of $40,000 a year. The judge gasped as he read out loud the details of their earning power, but

George reassured his partner that their relative wealth should not prejudice the outcome. Their case does not concern money, it is related to their professional reputation, and all the arguments have been made on both sides. They sit together in silence and wait, and as they do so Bert steals a nervous glance at his resolute partner.

> Especially when set against the austere, and somewhat aloof Mr. Williams, it was clear that many regarded George Walker as little more than a bediamonded Lenox Avenue pimp for, among his many *transgressions*, it was said that the "chocolate drop" wore silk underwear at a time when most white Americans were still content to sport flannels. However, there was a deeply philosophical side to the man, and there was no doubt about his commitment to the negro race. A somewhat wistful Mr. Williams confirmed that it was in 1906 that his partner stated: "The one hope of the colored performer must be in making a radical departure from the old 'darky' style of singing and dancing . . . there is an artistic side to the black race, and if it could be properly developed on the stage, I believe the theatergoing public would profit much by it."

They sit together in silence and wait for the clerk of the court. If only there were some way to talk with Bert about his painful yearning for Eva. By doing so he might at least ease some of the burden from his own beleaguered person, but he senses his partner's disapproval of this woman in particular and so he says nothing. Bert stares down at his loosely clasped hands, which rest awkwardly on his knees, and George continues to sit silently in his partner's long shadow.

Lottie lives for the cherished moment in her sprawling day when she is able to secrete herself in the privacy of the bathroom. She closes in the door and perches on the edge of the enamel tub as the water chuckles from the faucets and the room fills with steam. She eases out of her robe and hangs it on the wooden hook inside the door and dips first one foot, and then the other, into the bathtub until she feels safe enough to slide herself down and under the surface of the water. She lies back and closes her eyes, all the while careful to keep her tightly coiled tufts of hair dry. She lies alone in the bathtub feeling beads of sweat emerge and then melt into her skin, seeing herself from above, imagining floating hair swimming out all around her. Every day, by herself for half an hour, emptying her mind of uncertainties and worries, and then slowly stepping clear of the water and draping her body in a thick towel and regally padding her way to her room, where, now clear of the water, she feels like a fish incapable of breathing. And then again tomorrow. The locked door and the chuckling water.

Lottie hopes that one night she might feel a cool tongue against her body, pulling lazy trails of saliva that will be massaged into her skin with the mouth and tongue working as one joyful unit, working slowly, slowly, fly-flicking tongue bruising her in the hollow of her neck don't stop don't yes breathe on me face down on me deeper and down hoping that she might wake up damp and exhausted and on the very edge of civilization bearing the gift of another person's body.

Her husband enters the bedroom and greets her with a counterfeit smile. He now refuses to take off his clothes in front of her. Mother, I'll be back. He ambles toward the bathroom clutching an armful of nightclothes, but as he leaves she wonders why he has bothered to abandon his library and return to their bedroom if his performance is to include this insult. She waits, and then he returns, fully covered and ready for sleep, and she understands that once again she will be denied even the most perfunctory of conversations. He does not seem to care that for her it is never really sleep as she is forced to tolerate the high drone of his breathing and privately suffer the pain of a heart that has felt the excitement of her marriage collapse into something that is more demeaning than mere boredom.

George sits in the leather armchair and listens to a pair of feet climbing stairs that he knows are crooked like unstraightened teeth, and then he hears the heavy sound of the lock turning in the door. Marshall has given her the spare key. She enters and stands before him, her cheeks overrouged, her legs slightly parted, her hands on her hips, her heavy scent hanging between them like a morning fog. To his eyes she is beautiful, a field of flowers that one might gaze upon from a fence, and he is happy for once again he is alone with her. He understands that she does not wish to hear his voice, and she cares little for his wit or his intelligence. He understands that she sees something else, but whatever it is that she sees he suspects that it is not George Walker. Eva pulls up her dress and fumbles for the top of her stockings. He watches and betrays interest. The second stocking is discarded and he stands and goes to her, his hands snaking down her sides before slipping around her so that he can clutch her back and pull her close to him. He inserts his fingers into the untamed mass of curls and pulls his hand like a rough comb and tugs her down onto a wooden chair so he can lean over and press himself into her and push firmly. He wrestles with her as her whole body arches and the words begin to fall from her lips yes Christ yes and he tries now to picture what they must look like, but she shudders and begins to talk to him George and in his mind Ada is nowhere to be found only Eva and as he races faster she begins now to moan at first softly George yes George more George, and a guilty George sees himself as Bert must see him but he can't stop and why should he stop for he loves Eva and Eva loves him and now the tight high-pitched squeal in her throat yes George and a scream and his hand races to clamp her mouth but she bites and he cries in pain and she gasps and breathes quickly but her breath is soon stilled and frozen for the motion is becoming more frenzied and he pushes harder until everything breaks Christ yes yes and she kicks out and knocks over a small table and as he falls back she slides forward on the chair and her voluminous dress billows in the air and settles about her waist exposing her to his eyes in a way more shocking than the act they have just participated in and he closes his eyes and stands in an imaginary circle of shame knowing that he hangs foolishly, embarrassed by the evidence of his lack of self-control, recognizing that again she has seen what she wished to see and he has failed.

Lying next to her he is filled with remorse. Ada, his wife. Dark star, dancer. Her small breasts are now no more than two stubborn buds that appear to be no longer either sensitive or inviting, and his stiff body stiffens further at her accidental touch, but he knows that her depressed soul has long ago learned to live with this hurt. Lying uncomfortably next to his wife he knows that in a few hours he will witness light filtering through the thin drapes as dawn breaks and the gloomy shadows will start inevitably to define themselves; first the wardrobe, then the chair, then the chest of drawers. Ada. Dark star by which he set a false course.

Prejudice means that, of course, we can never fall in love or have a romance at the center of our Williams and

Walker productions. It is all too easy for a colored show to offend a white audience so instead we pretend that we have no such emotions, and we are all guilty of this pretense, all of us. We accept that the remotest suspicion of a love story will condemn us to ridicule, but my husband, Mr. George Walker, he is trying to change this situation and I am right behind him in his efforts. There are ten thousand things we must think of every time we make a step and I am not sure that the public is fully aware of the limitations which other persons have made on us.

AIDA WALKER

Those shaded show girls are led by Aida Walker who used to be Ada Overton. Is the change from "Ady" to "I-e-da" meant to mark a musical advance by Williams and Walker from Negro melody to operatic music? Aida is a lively lightweight, impish, sprightly, and coquettish. Her complexion is half-tone and her hair hesitates between Marcel waves and Afric kinks.

PHILADELPHIA INQUIRER

KINKY

Introduced by Aida Overton Walker

Kinky, Kinky your skin is kind o' inky,
But I love you I do,
Shady maybe but a perfect lady

Ev'ry inch of you
Kinky, Kinky there's a little dinky hut
Just built for us two,
Tarry, marry and it's there I'll carry you my Kinky True.
True.

Having settled their dispute with their former promoter, George stands on a simple wooden chair and addresses the company. His gestures are neat and confident and he punches the air to make his points. Bert looks up at his partner and realizes that George is committed to every word that he is saying. George believes that they are about to change American theater. He believes that *Abyssinia* will be ten times the success that *In Dahomey* was. He believes that the day has come for the Negro to storm the American stage and stake his claim to a position of equality alongside his fellow white performers. He believes that Williams and Walker are giving America both culture and history, and the introduction of Americanized African songs is helping to begin this process of moving away from the old darky stereotype. Slouch Negroes are no longer acceptable. Hell, I ain't nobody's uncle, and I ain't called Tom, cries his partner. George believes, but Bert wonders why George has chosen not to speak with him about his beliefs.

All that was expected of a colored performer was singing and dancing and a little storytelling. . . . [White performers] used to make themselves look as ridiculous as they could when portraying a "darky" character. In their "make up" they always had tremendously big red lips and their costumes were frightfully exaggerated. The one fatal result of this to the colored performers was that they imitated the white performers in their make-up as "darkies."

Dancing in the Dark

Nothing seemed more absurd than to see a colored man
making himself ridiculous in order to portray himself.

GEORGE WALKER

George moves toward the conclusion of his speech now, taking
them through their own history. Farewell, Tambo and Bones,
white men with blackened faces acting out their fantasy of the
colored race. Farewell, Jim Dandy, drunken creature of impulse,
dancing wildly, putting on airs, racially incapable of self-control.
Farewell the forlorn-looking indulgent black, with gross lips, and
eyes and legs that move independently of each other. No more
"Ethiopian Delineators," "Sons of Momus," or "Happy Plantation Darkies." George insists that *In Dahomey* has carried them
far beyond this, far beyond tambourines and banjos. George
insists that they are performers, they are artists, and he expects
them to carry themselves as such, and behave with the dignity
that is their calling at this point in their history. George insists
that America expects.

Later, when the company has dispersed, Bert resolves to remind
his partner that indeed they are performers, but it is the paying
audience, and not George's mythical America, that expects. Mr.
Booker T. Washington and Mr. W. E. B. DuBois exist for the
purposes of agitation and revolution for the colored race, but Mr.
Bert Williams and Mr. George Walker are entertainers, and they
have to respect the conventions of the time or face the conse-
quences. It is right and proper that Williams and Walker should
develop progressive new material and new dances, but they
should also remember that there are many others who are eager to
take their place. Too much fighting talk is not going to help anybody, and have not things already improved? They are not doing

buck and wing dances or breakdowns anymore, and they are slowly cakewalking their way into history with a talent that has been seared and trained for the stage. He will remind George that it is through hard work and application that Mr. Bert Williams has developed his timing to the point where he knows how to delay and hold back. The audience may think they are watching a powerless man but they are, in fact, watching art. We must understand how to make them feel safe, George. We must see the line. We cross that line, George, then who is going to pay to see us? They feel safe watching a supposedly powerless man playing an even more powerless thing. Williams and Walker have to respect this and simply strive to be the center of laughter, not the object of it. In time an alternative to the counterfeit colored culture that besmirches our stage will emerge, but only in time. Right now nobody will pay to see the colored man be himself, so we must tread carefully. This kind of talk is not going to help anybody, George. It's just feel-good talk for the company, nothing more to it than that. Later, when the company has dispersed, Bert will remind his partner of the reality of the situation.

This may sound snobbish, though it isn't; I'm not a native of the United States, but a West Indian, and I must take solace from my philosophy so long as I can earn my livelihood in this country. The rebellion is all out of me, for I know that it is up to me, and that this is the only civilization in the world where a man's color makes a difference, other matters being regarded as equal. You must admit that there's food for thought, not necessarily bitter, in the fact that in London I may sit in open lodge with a premier of Great Britain, and be entertained in the home of a distinguished novelist, while here in the United States, which fought four years for a certain principle, I am often treated with an air of personal condescension by the gentleman who sweeps out my dressing room, or the gentleman whose duty it is to turn the spot light on me, if the stage directions call upon him to do.

BERT WILLIAMS

But after Bert diplomatically reminds an unusually quiet George of the reality of the situation as he sees it, he asks his silent friend to help him figure out another question. George, you ever ask yourself why a white man would want to blacken his face with cork, dress down a point or two beneath the lowest of his race, and jig and dance around and pretend he's a colored man? I mean, try and walk like him, talk like him, make gestures, laugh, strike poses, behave just like how he imagines a colored man does. The fact is they do not like us, George, and they choose not to eat, drink, or live with colored folks, yet they must have some part of themselves that *wants* to be like us. But not like us truly, but some approximation of us; a strange creature of boundless appetite that they imagine to be us. Tell me, George, why do they want to be like us? But George is still thinking about something else.

The dressing room is where I dress, but it is also the place where I can set my true self to one side and put on the clothes and mind of another. A man I think I know, but despite what I tell George when the two of us are alone, the more I look at the modern world, the fewer of these men I discern. But the audience expects to see this man, and each night in my dressing room I have to find him, breathe life into him, make him walk, and talk, and grin. A wistful, sad, helpless man, but there is no doubt that the audience recognizes him. I slide one finger into the jar and work up a countenance that suggests the triumph of black velvet over my own light ebony. In my dressing room night will triumph over day. I watch my skin become black. But this is not me. Surely the audience understands this. This is simply a person that I have discovered, a person the audience claims to recognize.

And finally George speaks, but he is careful to keep his urgent voice low. Listen to me, Bert, the so-called character that you're playing is a damn-fool creature who has been created by the white man, and this "smoke" fixes us in their minds as helpless failures. But times have changed now and we should no longer be standing up in front of the white man and delivering simplistic stories with the right amount of darky naivete. I mean, let me ask you, how many of our own people are truly happy to just eat watermelon, or fall over on their faces, or mispronounce the English language? Time to put the cork to one side, Bert. White people are laughing at you, and colored folks in the audience are only laughing to keep from crying. Who is this darky that you give them, Bert? This fool who is easily duped into idiotic schemes, with his gross stories, and jokes on himself? Who is this man whose laziness is such that he only stirs to life when somebody mentions a ghost? This pork-eating, chicken-loving, fat-lipped, big-bellied lover of food who wants to hear music that's either melancholy, or something that he can jig to with big-foot, clumsy dancing. I told you already, not now, Bert. Not in the twentieth century. You gotta leave that man behind where he belongs, and it don't matter a damn how much you want to talk about what you do as art, I'm telling you, please cut that colored fool loose.

George announces to the press that *Abyssinia* will finally open in New York City on February 20, 1906. He informs them that it will be a musical play in four scenes set in Addis Ababa, in Abyssinia, featuring a cast of one hundred performers, spectacular lighting effects, elegant costumes, a market scene, a waterfall, and live animals. Bert Williams will play Jasmine Jenkins and George Walker will play Rastus Johnson. An excited George explains that the drama concerns the pair of them escorting a group of colored Americans back to the barbaric splendor of Africa, where they encounter both adventure and danger in a plot that explores the theme of mistaken identity. However, when the production finally opens George is outraged at the critics' opinion that the production is too long, and they declare that in large part the whole spectacle is pretentious and overblown, and that the live animals steal what is effectively little more than a *pageant*. Eventually, after thirty-one performances, their disappointed producer claims bankruptcy and the show, being far too expensive to maintain, quickly closes. Sadly, *Abyssinia* fails to be the artistic and creative breakthrough that George, in particular, so desperately craves, but what aggravates him the most is the claim of the vast majority of the so-called *critics* that *Abyssinia*'s greatest failure is that it contains far too little of the colored coon Mr. Bert Williams presenting his celebrated corkface routines.

Aida tries to speak with Lottie, but the more tight-lipped Lottie becomes, the more Aida opens up until Aida eventually tells her what she realizes her friend probably already knows. George and the wild white girl. She knows about this, doesn't she? Lottie nods slowly, understanding that she will have to confess, otherwise the conversation can go no further. Has Lottie ever met the woman with George? Lottie shakes her head and wonders if Aida has forgotten that she has done what Bert wished and retired from the stage. Lottie's theatrical circle is shrinking. Has Lottie ever spoken to the woman? Again she shakes her head. The two colored women fall silent. Aida seldom walks the few blocks to visit with her, so when Lottie opened the door and saw the clearly sleep-deprived Aida standing before her she knew that something serious was troubling her friend. Aida has chosen her time well for the house is quiet and Lottie is alone. Does Bert know about the woman? To this Lottie can honestly answer that she does not know. Has Bert said anything to her about George? There is no reason for her to admit that conversations between herself and Bert are probably even less satisfactory than those between Aida and George. There is no need for her to divulge that she long ago learned not to probe the closed mind of her strange second husband. No, Bert has said nothing to her about George. He has said nothing to her about anything. He keeps himself to himself. She smiles at Aida, whose hurt is both public and private, but she has no advice to offer the poor woman, who, luckily, does not appear to be asking for any. So she decides to offer Aida some tea, and Aida nods and then, remembering her manners, she smiles.

Aida has been circling the Harlem streets for two hours, peering intently through the windows of various bars and cafés, loitering outside of the barbershops, even looking in the churches, but he is nowhere to be found. She is careful to make sure that her body language does not suggest that she is harboring any unease, but it is not until she begins to pass the same people for a second, and then a third time, their puzzled faces eloquent, that she eventually realizes that it is time for her to go home and wait in the privacy of their apartment.

Alone in bed, with the drapes drawn back. The unbearable lucidity of insomnia descends upon Aida. As night reaches, and then passes, its perfect pitch, she watches the slow light begin to bleed through the black; then through the blue-black; and then finally flood the sky. A new day.

Dancing in the Dark

Lottie feels guilty, for she failed to offer her friend any form of
comfort or support. She has always known Aida to be a confident, unbreakable woman, and up until this moment her role has
been to step aside and let Aida become Aida, and not interfere
with her friend's desire for attention, and her quest for fame. But
something has gone terribly wrong. Shortly before dawn, before
daylight streaks the sky, Lottie rolls from her empty bed and proceeds to put on her robe.

Tonight Metheney's is quiet and he sits in his corner, after his
performance, after his day is done. He thought about buying
flowers, or some chocolates, a gift of some kind to rekindle the
bond between himself and his wife, but unable to decide exactly
what he should purchase, he chooses, in the end, to buy nothing.
These days Mother looks at his books the way he imagines a jealous wife looks at another woman. It might be easier if she could
find the words and say something to him, but so far she has chosen to remain silent. George, on the other hand, continues both to
talk and to agitate, and he has informed his partner that he
intends to form a social organization of Negro entertainers; he
has also spoken to Bob Cole and Ernest Hogan and to some of
the other performers, but of late things have not been easy
between Williams and Walker and their colleagues, who, jealous
of the well-established prominence of the Williams and Walker
team, have begun to question their talent and commitment to the
race. In fact, since the closure of *Abyssinia* things have not always
been easy between Williams and Walker. Clyde D places another
drink before him, but as ever, he says nothing to Mr. Williams.
The dreams have returned and he cannot sleep. Last night he
once again chose to sleep on the sofa in his library, but the noise
of traffic in the street was distracting and he found it difficult to

rest. Scrape off the black. This strange phrase circling in his mind. Scrape off the black. And in the morning his wife entered the library with the newspaper in one hand and a robe tied tightly at the waist, and as she set down the newspaper she looked through her husband as though he was not present. He wanted to talk to her, but he understands that in order to do so he will have to travel west and then east and then south, and back to a place and to a time when he was not yet two people. The one pitying the other.

Under the chuckling water I can see nothing, I can hear nothing, and I can feel nothing. Except, of course, heat. I am warm and I feel the rush of hot blood pumping through my twice-married body. Eventually I lift my head clear out of the water, and narrow my eyes. A crazy wash of white everywhere, and steam. I feel dizzy, but these days I prefer peering at the world through half-open eyes.

The bathroom is full of strange people who stare at me. But how is this possible? I live here. Why are these people looking down at me as though I have carried out some act of which I ought to feel ashamed? No, I am not ashamed. Leave. Please leave my bathroom. All except my husband. Where is my husband? My father-in-law places a hand upon my arm. I know who he is, I am not stupid. I recognize my father-in-law for he is the only other man in my life, but he too must leave. Where is my husband? I feel my father-in-law's grip tighten and I push him from me. His wife catches him before he tumbles to the ground. Where is *my* husband?

Are you all right, Mother? My husband leans over me. His face is gentle and kind, like it used to be when we sat in the small, concrete park in the dark shadow cast by the solitary tree. I can see that he cares, but I cannot speak. Bert, I know your heart is heavy with problems that you feel you cannot share with me. I understand. My poor husband. A new husband, different from Mr. Thompson, and the whole world appears to sit heavily on this sad man's broad shoulders. Perhaps if he could see me in the water, perhaps if he could see me underneath the water, then he would understand that hot blood still pumps through my body, that I am still in his life. I have not left. I have gone nowhere. I swear this was not an attempt to drown myself, it was an accident. I can lift the world for him. I can lift the world for you, Bert. Perhaps if he saw me in the bathtub then he would come to bed at night. This is all I ask, that he begin again by sharing a bed with me at night.

I have no desire to be like Aida. I have no desire to discover myself dancing with increasing fury. Shamed, and finding life impossible and still so young. I wish to travel through life with my husband by my side. The two of us walking hand in hand and moving gently, but purposefully, toward my husband's goals. This is all I wish for. This alone would satisfy me. Aida with dark circles under her eyes, abandoned on 132nd Street, undone by the whiteness of winter. Between us two husbands straying, one in mind, one in body, although it is unclear to me which is the greater betrayal. A long time since the photograph, the four of us, each in our own way excited, each in our own way consumed by nerves. Tension shooting through us like gunshots. I watched the man move them around. Hold it. And now this way and hold it. My handsome Bert. I cried the first time I saw him perform.

Shut the door, Lottie. Thank you. It helps keep out the cold. And you know you don't have to stand on no ceremony with me. Take a seat, girl, and thank you for stopping by. And I'm glad you're

feeling better after fainting in the tub like that. Lottie, I see
George at the show same as you do, but that's about all for I don't
seem to be able to find him up here in Harlem. Seems like everybody else knows where to find him. I know, Marshall's. But I hear
that place ain't what it used to be, and that it's fixing to close
down. It troubles me that he would be wasting his time down
there. I'm sorry, I haven't even offered you a drink. You sure?
Things haven't got to the stage where I don't know how to entertain, but you must tell me if I ever get that way. If I ever get so bad
that I lose my manners. Now that would be a sad situation, don't
you think? Well, if you're sure. Did Bert talk to you about how
things are? With George, I mean. You know it's not in my nature
to pry, but I'm just wondering if things are fine between himself
and George. I got no reason to think otherwise, but I suppose the
truth is I'm just looking for clues. Just looking for something to
help me understand what's become of my own life. I think
George loves me, Lottie. No, that isn't true. I know he loves me,
but it just makes everything that much harder to understand.
Why so bold? Why not creep around a little like most of them?
Why does he have to do me like that, Lottie? What have I done
to him to make him do me like that? No, you only just got here.
No, please. Sit. Or maybe we can take a walk together? But don't
leave me just yet. You know, I got liquor if it's liquor you're needing. Lottie. What's happening, Lottie?

Two o'clock in the afternoon and Aida is sitting in the window
seat held spellbound by the winter storm. Outside the snow is still
falling and the naked trees are standing to attention, and as the
snowstorm strengthens in intensity it becomes more alluring. She
watches the flakes buzzing wildly in the early afternoon light, and
she notices passersby protecting their faces, scared of being cut by
the whirling blades of sleet. She gently arches her neck and takes

the morphine straight from the bottle, a smile on her face, the sound of a waterfall in her ears, and she looks forward to a new dawn. She has covered all the mirrors with drapes so that she can travel through what remains of this winter day without being seen.

George bursts into Metheney's and rushes over to him. He looks up, and because his friend's waistcoat is exactly level with his eyes he can see that it is uncharacteristically spotted with food. The rest of his costume is unmarked. Pants, jacket, cravat, spats, this is dapper George with his diamond rings and matching stickpins. This is the Bon Bon Buddy. George blocks what little light leaks through the begrimed windows. Bert gestures to his partner to sit down, but George remains standing with his mouth hanging imprudently half open. Something is wrong but he waits for George to unburden himself. He has no desire to force the issue in any way, but George simply stands and looks down at him and he sees the clouds beginning to roll behind his friend's eyes. He reaches up and takes George's clammy hand into his own.

He looks around the crowded and chaotic hospital waiting room and it occurs to him that it must always be like this. After all, people get sick without regard to the time of day or night. George has talked incessantly all the way to the hospital, but now, as they wait in the airless room, he seems to have become a little calmer. I guess the accident is my fault and I got to change. He looks at George, who leans forward and rests his elbows on his knees and then, cupping his hands, he drops his tired chin into the ten-fingered basket. I got to start looking out for my Aida, and I guess I don't have much choice in the matter. Anything happens to her on account of me, then it's just going to bring disgrace on all of us. Bert looks at his distressed partner and slowly nods, and then he turns from his friend and listens as George begins to jabber idly to himself with his newly pronounced lisp.

Aida appears to be peaceful. She is draped in white with her eyes shut tightly against the electric light, and her thin arms on top of the hospital sheet and straight like two dark arrows. She looks like an angel, and George cannot take his eyes from her. The doctor encourages him to move forward, and so he pulls up a chair and sits and stares as though he is gazing upon his wife for the first time.

Alone at night, outside the hospital, Bert decides to walk home through the wintry streets, and under a sky that is choked with stars. From a fire escape, a few stories above his head, a huge chunk of ice plunges to the sidewalk and explodes in a constellation of crystal bullets. He stands frozen for a moment, his breath clouding in the frosty air, and then he continues on his route, carefully picking his way through the slush so that the melted snow does not climb up and into his shoes. He keeps the brim of his hat low, but glances at the street-lamp faces of those who hurry by at this midnight hour. Near the corner of Fifth Avenue he sees a single early daffodil laboring under the weight of this late snow and he looks around himself and then stoops to pluck it. He will give this to his wife, who he knows will be unable to find any sleep until her troubled husband returns home safely.

Bert sleeps next to his grateful wife. In the morning Mother brings an orange to the bed, and then the newspaper. She asks whether he thinks she ought to visit with Aida, but he assures her that Aida will be fine. George is attending to her. Mother's mouth falls open, for she cannot disguise her surprise, but she says nothing. He opens the newspaper, but as soon as his wife leaves the room he rests it down.

Having eaten the orange, he climbs from the bed, gets dressed, and walks the few blocks through the soot-blackened snow down to George and Aida's place, where he finds his partner sitting alone and smoking a cigar. George greets him warmly and then announces that he must soon leave for he has to go back to the hospital and visit his wife. He stutters as he reminds Bert what a fine dancer Aida is, and how she is the real star of the company. He asks Bert what he thinks of her number "I'll Keep a Warm Spot in My Heart for You," telling him that it was undoubtedly the high point in *Abyssinia* and that maybe in the future they ought to feature Aida and her dancers more prominently. Didn't she put the dance numbers together better than anything in a Cole and Johnson show, better than anything Hogan had ever done? "Menelik's Tribute to Queen Tai Ta," "The Dance of the Falasha Maids," and "The Dance of the Amhara Maids." Who had ever seen choreography like it? George talks, and Bert listens for George likes to talk. George also likes to be right more than any man he has ever met, but he is not right about Aida. She is not the star of the show, nor does she need to be featured more prominently. Aida simply needs a husband, that is all. If she had a husband, then everything would be all right, and good things might well follow from this. But Aida is lying alone in a hospital room while a guilt-burdened George smokes a cigar and talks incessantly to his partner.

George lights another cigar. He stands now and begins to pace back and forth by the window. He insists that their new show, *Bandana Land*, will be decidedly different, something their public has never seen before. An impatient George stubs out the newly lit cigar, and then he speaks quietly. But let me get this clear, you're saying that because white folks pay to see us we got to please them, right? Bert nods, for he knows that this is the truth, and although he does not like this fact it nonetheless remains a fact. George takes a seat opposite his partner. George appears to have forgotten that his wife is lying alone in a hospital bed and he is supposed to be visiting with her. But I'm tired of pleasing white folks, Bert. I'm tired and beat. There is a strange lisp to George's tongue. Bert, a man can kill himself trying to please white folks.

—Your wife getting strong again, honey? I hear she's the star of the new show?
—I don't know about star.
—You getting good early notices, George?
—From you?
—You better save your strength with all that talking if you're looking for good notices from me.
—I hear Jimmie's soon going to close down the hotel.
—Well, Eva'll find some other place for us to play. This ain't the only joint in town.
—I guess not.
—What's the matter, you don't want to play no more, is that it? You feeling guilty, George?
—I ain't feeling no guilt.
—Well don't you think you should?
—Whose side are you on here?
—You better change that tone, Mr. High and Mighty George Walker. That ain't no way to treat a lady, now is it? Well, is it?
—Eva.
—I can hear you. You fixing to end things between us, George? After all this time?

—Eva, she's not doing so well.

—Now, that's not what I asked you, George Walker. If Jimmie closes down the hotel it just means that we don't have a roost at this flophouse, but there's plenty of other places. Damn, we can even buy a place, now wouldn't that be swell? A furnished place, maybe up in Harlem . . .

—No.

—No? George, you better get whatever it is that's on your mind out into the open before I lose my patience with you. What's the matter with you? You listening to me, George Walker?

> Gentlemen of the Thirteen Club—I have seen in the daily press an announcement of a dinner to take place at the Harlem Casino Café this evening the 13th of February, 1908, [at] which time representatives of the Hebrew race, the Japanese race, the Italian race, and the Irish race will speak on the subject, "Is Race Prejudice a Form of Superstition?" Gentlemen, please explain how it came to pass that your learned society failed to invite a representative of my race to speak at your dinner. Is it possible that you have members who are seeking to emancipate themselves from superstition and yet they fail to be broad[-minded] enough to ask a man of African blood in his veins to be present and to take part in your deliberations? . . . Gentlemen, please do not misunderstand me in the least. I am not a race agitator, and do not claim to thoroughly understand the questions with which your society deals. Williams and Walker seek to make people happy by giving them a clean-cut show, composed of and acted entirely by members of the African race.

> GEORGE WALKER

She talks endlessly, but her tirade is really a series of suggestions and complaints loosely strung together and punctuated with gestures, some decent, the remainder an unsubtle appeal to his baser instincts. She insists that men have tried to use her before, but they have failed for she is "hotter than Tabasco." She laughs out loud, but George starts in and explains to her that these things run their course, and he can't live with the thought of bringing disgrace on his race should anything happen to Aida, but Eva isn't prepared to listen. She stomps around the room, tossing back her head like a petulant pony, running her hands through her untamed hair, and spitting out her foul words and kicking the furniture. By the time she finally decides to leave he has long stopped listening to her. The slamming of the door shakes the whole room and only serves to remind him of why they call her "the cyclone." He goes to the window and discreetly pulls the drape to one side so that he can look down onto Fifty-third Street, where a clearly distressed Eva is walking slowly and with her head lowered. As he gazes down at her he is surprised to feel tears pooling behind his eyes.

Lottie opens the door and informs George that her husband is at Metheney's Bar. George tips his hat and graciously thanks his friend's visibly aging wife, but decides that he won't disturb Bert. There will be time enough to set things straight with his partner tomorrow. He would want to know. Not that he would ever ask, but he feels obliged to tell Bert that this particular chapter has come to an end.

Eva took out a full-page advertisement in all the theatrical newspapers making it clear that if anybody had the temerity to accuse her of having had relations with a well-known, but unnamed, colored performer, then she would sue. She claimed that she was aware of certain unpleasant rumors that were circulating regarding her personal behavior, but she urged her fans to use their intelligence in distinguishing between her stage persona and the Christian moral strictures within which she lived her daily life. She pointed out that she was a happily married woman, and such slander besmirched not only her personal and professional reputation, but that of her loving spouse. The advertisement was featured prominently, as were the news reports that picked up on its appearance. In response she received only favorable notices, all of which praised her courage in distancing herself from such abominable talk. As a result she was received with renewed affection and the "I Don't Care Girl" enjoyed a sudden upsurge of popularity.

Bert continues to perform nightly in the new Williams and Walker production, *Bandana Land,* but he does so with a weary spirit for the experience of *Abyssinia* appears to have taught George very little. His erratic partner seems even more determined than ever to make a pageant as opposed to offering a coherent production, but Bert decides against trying to talk with George for he knows that his words will have little, if any, effect. It is clear, not only to Bert but to others, including Mother, that artistically speaking the two men are moving in different directions for Bert's queer clothes and quaint colored humor contrasts bizarrely with the bejeweled opulence of George's vision. Sadly, the two partners no longer share the same stage with ease for George's desire for swell grace and romance makes no sense when set against Bert's old-fashioned imitation of a nigger coon.

He continues to soap the man's face, all the while looking closely at his client's features, until he loses sight of the individual beneath the white foam. He sharpens his razor on the strop and then makes a few small movements of his wrist as though carving the air into thin slices. A seated customer suddenly exclaims, "Don't you know it's the man's son you're talking about?" He tries not to listen to their gossip as he gives the razor a few final strokes against the strop, but what can he do? He knows that this is a barbershop, and that a barbershop is a colored man's country club, where folks feel free to run their mouths in all directions, but his Bert has bought the shop for him, and in spite of everything, he has his loyalties to his son. This being the case, he knows that eventually he'll have to say something to these crispy-haired American men for they cannot talk about his West Indian son and expect a big man like Fred Williams to endure much more of this discourtesy. Next comes the water. He likes to rinse his hands one final time before touching a man's skin, and so he lets the warm water ribbon gently through his fingers. All the boy is trying to do is entertain people; he is trying to make them happy and make them laugh, but the truth is he has never been able to watch his son perform beyond that first time. He takes up the towel and dries his hands as another customer gets his point across. "Making us all look foolish, don't care what nobody says, the nigger makes us all look bad." He takes the razor and drags it gently across his client's face, careful to ensure that his strokes are smooth and true. How many more of these conversations? Damn it, this is his son, and people should respect this, and appreciate the fact that Williams and Walker is an all-Negro organization that employs coloreds and gives them a chance to succeed, and often presents them with a start in the entertainment business. However, whichever way you look at it, a barbershop is not a good place to frequent if you don't wish to hear talk, and soon Fred Williams had heard enough talk. Eventually everybody knew the story of what happened on the morning Fred Williams finally closed down his barbershop, but nobody ever heard the story from Fred. In fact, according to Billy "Too Fine" Thomas, after Fred was through with his craziness he just took off his smock, tossed it over the back of one of those big old padded leather chairs, and locked the door behind him. Billy "Too Fine" Thomas worked with Fred in the shop as some kind of apprentice, doing the easy cuts, wiping down the counters, and sweeping up hair from the floor, and for years after Fred Williams's patience finally ran out, Billy could ride three or four free drinks in any bar in Harlem on the back of his story—a story that got bigger with every retelling.

"You see, that morning I knowed something was wrong with Fred for I could smell the whiskey on his breath, but Fred ain't no liquor head and it wasn't like Fred at all, and then when he starts to organize his scissors and blades and everything, he's banging things down like he's spoiling for a fight and I figure something must have happened at home with the wife, for most of the worriments that trouble a man go right back to the wife, and most likely he's dealing with some kind of problem behind closed doors that he got to play out in public, so I don't say nothing and I swear I just try to stay out of the nigger's way and so I go through to the back and try to reckon up how I'm going to survive this day, but in the end I know I just gotta watch carefully and see what old Fred does with that temper of his for the man's just crashing around like a crazy fool, and then when I come back through there's a customer sitting high up in the chair, been in a few times, but he ain't no regular, and I don't even know the man's name, but already I see that blade going back and forth, back and forth, and then I see the blood for Fred's cut the man, cut him good, but it's like Fred don't notice or something, so I move toward Fred and just at that moment the man cries out in pain, I mean his cheek is cut good and proper, and now the man can feel the blood beginning to trickle down his face, all hot and flowing, and so he raises his hand and touches his face, then he looks at his hand and he's fierce angry, shouting and cussing, and just when I'm about to put my hand on Fred's arm to tell him, 'Hey, Fred, the man's bleeding,' I'll be damned if the island nigger doesn't turn and cut me too, doesn't say a word to me, just a quick movement of his wrist and I'm holding on to my arm and blood pumping through it like I sprung a leak and so I look at the man with blood on his face, and me with blood on my arm, and right there and then I know that old Fred's come unglued and so me and the customer start to back away from him and move toward the door, all the while keeping an eye on that blade for we both know that anything can happen with Fred for it's clear that he ain't through with his cutting for the day, but we both hightail it out of there and leave him to wait for whoever else is dumb enough to venture into Fred Williams's barbershop, but I know right away that I'm going to have to get me another job, either in barbering or something else, but I don't much care what it is as long as I don't have to work with this crazy man for the devil had surely seized old Fred's soul and good sense had jumped clear out of the man's head."

George knocks at the door and waits. He holds on to the railing for his head is spinning, but the news of his new social organization will soon be made public and it is important that he formally invite Bert to participate, for he knows that Bert can be a mighty formal kind of a man. George looks around and notices a few people staring up at him as he stands at the top of the flight of steps. They know who he is, and the tasty suit leaves them in no doubt. He waves and they smile, and then the door opens and a grim-faced Lottie ushers him in and she announces that Bert is in his library keeping company with his books. She speaks with a strange mixture of both pride and contempt, but he has heard this tone before and he therefore tries his best to ignore it. Lottie and Aida remain friends, and this being the case he seldom says more to Lottie than is absolutely necessary, but he knows exactly what she thinks of him. He only has to see the way she looks him up and down, as though inspecting him for some external evidence of the inner taint that she obviously feels disfigures his personality.

Bert rests the book in his lap and looks up as his wife withdraws and leaves the two men alone.
—Everything all right?
—Figured I'd just come by and talk to you for a minute about the social organization.
—Won't you take a seat?
George nods and carefully closes in the door behind him, but try as he might he cannot disguise the fact that his legs are shaking and his gait is unsteady.

An organization to be known as the "Frogs" was formed Sunday evening at the residence of George W. Walker, 107 West 132nd Street. The prime movers in forming such an organization are the leading actors of the race, and it is the intention of the incorporators to make the "Frogs" to the Negro performer, as well as to the members of the race, what the Lambs' Club and the Players' Club mean to the white profession. . . . The Frogs have been formed for social, historical and library purposes with a view to promoting social intercourse between the representative members of the Negro theatrical profession and to those connected directly or indirectly with art, literature, music, scientific and liberal professions and the patrons of arts.

NEW YORK AGE

He sits in Bert's library and looks at his friend and wonders if
Bert even remembers those nights in the mountains of Colorado.
They had dreams back then, and they were determined and
talked often of the future, but these days Bert never speculates
about the future. In fact, these days Bert seems reluctant to talk
on any subject, and he hardly ever mentions *Bandana Land*. Bert
appears to have effectively passed business responsibility to
George, for he does not seem in the slightest bit interested in
either Williams and Walker or the Frogs, and for some time now
George has felt that they *ought* to talk frankly but he knows that
Bert is uncomfortable sharing his feelings. George understands
that the situation with his father must be making life even more
difficult for his partner, for people are talking, and the more
people talk, the less poor Bert seems to want to open up. Of late,
Bert seldom leaves his home unless he is going to the theater, or
unless he is visiting Metheney's, but George suspects that, in his
mind, Bert travels.

> I used to go over [to Europe] every summer and study
> pantomime from Pietro, the great pantomimist. He is the
> one artist from whom I can truthfully say that I learned.
> He taught me gesture, facial expression—without which
> I would not have been able to do the poker game stunt
> that was so popular. . . . I played a good deal of pan-
> tomime in Europe. I did the Toreador in the pantomime
> version of *Carmen* and many other parts.
>
> BERT WILLIAMS

But George knows that Bert travels only in his mind.

> The poker game was the most famous stage act that
> Mr. Williams ever performed, and I had read that he

included it for the first time in *Bandana Land* where he played the part of Skunton Bowser, who takes up the deck of cards while heavily under the influence of apple-jack. I wanted to ask Mr. Williams about the origins of the act, for he claimed to have discovered his technique for the routine while studying with "Pietro" in Europe. However, although I read everything that I could find, I found it impossible to discover anything about this Mr. Pietro. Even more puzzling was the fact that nobody I questioned had any memory of Mr. Williams ever doing any studying in Europe. When I found myself privileged to be sitting opposite Mr. Williams I had second thoughts about raising this puzzling quandary. Instead, I asked him about the big hit song of the show, "Late Hours," which he sung while performing the famous poker game routine. Mr. Williams was happy to talk to me about the song.

The hard-drinking man gratefully accepted another whiskey from George and then settled back to tell his late-night tale. "You see," he began, "I hear Mr. Bert got the idea while the two of you were playing in Lincoln, Nebraska, some time back. Seems like he went to see an old friend in the hospital and the guard said to him, 'Would you like to walk around with me and see the place?' Mr. Bert accepted the invitation and the guard first took him to see the patients that were almost ready to leave the hospital. Then the guard took him to another part of the hospital where the patients were very ill. Apparently there was one fellow in a room alone. Evidently, his mental illness was due to gambling, playing poker. In his room was a table and a chair, and the fellow was in there all alone, talking to himself and acting as though he were in a poker game, for he would go through the motions of having a drink, looking around the table, and smiling at the other players. He would reach in his imaginary pile of chips and throw in his ante, looking around to see if everybody was in, then smile again. He would shuffle and begin to deal around and after he had finished dealing, he would pick up his imaginary hand and look at each player after they had discarded, to see how many cards they wanted. All this time he would have a smile on his face as if he believed he had the best hand, and as each player asked for cards, his smile would get broader, and he would put up fingers to show he understood how many. Then, when one of the imaginary players stood pat, his smile would begin to vanish. When the deal was all over, the betting would start. Each player would call or pass. When it was up to him, he would look at his hand, put it down, pour a little drink from his imaginary bottle, and look again. Then he would push in the last of his chips and call. After the showdown, he had the second-best hand. He would stand up, brush off his pants, and go back to his bunk, place his elbows on his knees, and, leaning on his hands, shake his head slowly. I reckon that it's from this fellow that your Mr. Bert learned that particular routine. I believe he picked up plenty by just watching ordinary folks. That's all. Just watching ordinary folks, then adding his own feel to it." George smiled and signaled to the barman to bring another whiskey.

Fred Williams opens his eyes and sees his American daughter-in-law standing before him with a glass of juice and a plate of toasted bread. The items are balanced on a tray that she cradles in her arms. She holds it like an offering, and he stares at her. No more barbering. She has made it clear that it is fine for him to stay in the house until he regains some peace in his mind, or until his wife returns from California, whichever occurs first, but his daughter-in-law is adamant that there must be no more cutting.

He looks at her and realizes that his boy has found himself a good woman, and then he closes his eyes and pretends that she isn't there, but he listens. He hears her put the tray down on the bedside table. For a moment she stands over him and he worries that she might say something, but she remains silent. He is grateful that his daughter-in-law does not lean over and try to touch him and gain his attention. He keeps his eyes firmly closed and listens as she leaves the room.

A heart heavy like a stone, for he now understands that bringing his son to America was an act of foolishness that has allowed the powerful nation in the north to come between them. The country has made a nigger of the boy and there is nothing that he can do to fight this United States of America, which he now understands habitually snatches children from the arms of those who gave them life and encourages them to become people who their parents no longer recognize, but people who their parents cannot stop loving even though they despise the transformation and resent the loss. A heart heavy like a stone, his handsome West Indian son a stage nigger in America, the boy's own heart leaden with guilt, his mouth stopped up, his words trapped in his head, unable to reach out to father or wife, deaf to everything but the roar of the white audience.

Tonight we go at each other as though we are animals tearing each other apart. She tries to devour me and I fight her off at the same time as I too try to devour her. Pushing at her, pulling back, and then pulling her on. The orchestra is warming up, playing runs, the blare of the trumpet, the gun rattle of the drums, and there is plenty of noise out there, enough to mask what is going on in dressing room number two with the chair thrust up against the door and the drapes pulled tight. I turn Eva to the side and push her down onto the floor. She tries to get up and I slap her and she cries out so I force my arm into her mouth and she bites the sleeve of my velvet jacket. Bitch. I spit the word at her and she growls at me. Bitch, I say again and a paw reaches out and slashes at my face and as I turn away a single nail catches me and instinctively my hand goes up. She's laughing now, and she tries to wrestle me off but I go at her and tear at her dress until it rips. I pull out first one breast and then the other, and then I see the fear in her eyes. Bitch. Cut me? Cut George Walker? I press Eva to the floor as though I'm trying to drive her into the basement of the theater. Down on her, pushing down on her until she stops struggling, and the sweat pops onto her brow, each bead independent, and she is defeated. The stage manager knocks at the door and I hear his raised voice. Mr. Walker. He knocks again. Okay, I'll be there. The sleeve of my jacket is ripped, gashed purple, and I stand up but Eva cannot move. I know that she is wounded, and I can see that her dress is torn and that she is in disarray, but I abandon her and look in the mirror. There is blood on my cheek. Mr. Walker, your call. I wipe the blood with my damaged sleeve and try to rearrange myself. Mr. Walker. She looks at me, her chest heaving with exhaustion, her eyes still hungry. I'll wait, she says. I'll be here. Mr. Walker, please, Mr. Williams is in the wings. I look at her and realize that I don't have the energy to argue.

"Bon Bon Buddy" by Walker went unusually well.

NEW YORK SUN

Bon Bon Buddy, the chocolate drop, dat's me,
Bon Bon Buddy, is all that I want to be;
I've gained no fame, but ain't ashamed

Dancing in the Dark

> I'm satisfied with my nickname,
> Bon Bon Buddy, the chocolate drop, dat's me.

He looks at George and can see that it is happening again. Something is wrong with George, but his partner is not talking to him about it. Once again, George is forgetting his lines.

> Bon Bon Buddy, the chocolate drop, dat's me,
> Bon Bon Buddy . . .

He wants to ask him, George, why are you looking at me like this? Staring at me as though you have seen a ghost. It is the third prompt that George has taken tonight, and his dancing is entirely graceless. He wants to ask his partner what he can do to help, but instead he looks on helplessly as George begins now to mutter the lyrics to himself.

> I've gained no fame, but I ain't ashamed
> I'm satisfied . . .

George?

But George is not listening. George is gazing into the middle distance as though he can see something that nobody else can see. I take his arm and make like it is part of the show. I pretend that I am taking pity on this poor deluded colored man dressed up as though he owns half the known world, and as I begin to guide George off the stage I try to create some humor. We both stumble for I have to show them that it does not matter how uppity a colored man chooses to dress, he will always be little more than some bumbling fool with no idea of how to control himself. Initially the audience is not sure what is happening, but they soon gain confidence and laughter ensues. I start to hurry now for George's whole weight is upon me and he is not stepping anymore, and I am dragging him like I am toting a large sack of potatoes. Somehow it does not seem right that we still have to be in the act, and then I see Aida waiting anxiously in the wings with a look on her face that suggests that she is about to scream. She reaches out her hands to help for I am struggling now as George has lost consciousness. As the stage manager brings down the curtain we are deafened by a storm of applause from the audience, who demand more.

I lay my partner down backstage and feel for his pulse, which, although weak, seems to obey a steady beat. However, before I can do anything further for George I have to remove my face. The stage manager has already called for the doctor, and Aida is propping up her husband's head, and so I excuse myself. I'll be back, Aida. I am unsure if she can hear me, but as I move off I notice that the stage manager is following me into the corridor. Mr. Williams? I turn and face the young man. Miss Tanguay. Before she left she asked if you'd let her know how things are. The stage manager pauses. With Mr. Walker, that is.

I look apprehensively into the mirror and make sure that I have removed every last trace of makeup, and only now do I carefully wash my hands and face. There is an impatient knocking at my dressing room door but I wait until I have toweled off before opening the door. A distraught Aida stands before me and I step to one side so that she can enter. She sits and looks around, and then she lowers her eyes. I know that despite her distress she has waited and given me time to make myself presentable. She looks up now and informs me that a worried-looking doctor is examining George, and he has just suggested to her that George is losing his health. It is difficult to know what to say in reply, so I say nothing, knowing that Aida must now find the courage to continue. She threads her hands together. What's the matter with him, Bert? George must have spoken to you about it. I asked the doctor but he said that as yet he doesn't know, but he was lying to me, wasn't he? I'm George's wife, and I've got a right to know. It ain't right that after all these years I should still be feeling that others know more about my husband than I do. I look directly at Aida, feeling the sting of her veiled accusation, but I remain as mystified about George's condition as she appears to be. This is his health, Bert, and it's important and I have to know. I understand, I say, but the doctor is the man best qualified to answer your questions. Aida lowers her eyes and begins to silently sob. I look away.

> According to Mr. Williams they were in Boston one night, and George Walker was performing "Bon Bon Buddy" when suddenly he began to drone out the lyrics in a thick-lipped manner. Apparently some of the cast members smiled because, to begin with, they believed that Mr. Walker was improvising a new gag, but Mr. Williams knew differently. It was only later that he, and the rest of the company, learned just how ill Mr. Walker was. In fact, he had actually suffered a stroke.

Aida continues to sob, but both she and Bert know that George will still insist on performing every night in *Bandana Land*. However, despite the optimistic bulletin that the Williams and Walker company will undoubtedly send out to the press in the morning, it is clear to Bert that George's health is beginning rapidly to deteriorate. The following week Bert instructs the costume department to prepare a George Walker outfit for Aida so that she can deputize in the event of another serious collapse of her husband's health.

At every theater on the road, George's dressing room is decorated with a huge display of roses, but there is never a card and Aida never quizzes her husband as to their origin.

In a rooming house in Chicago, a few days before Christmas, I sit downstairs with my wife and listen to Aida, who is upstairs singing gentle lullabies to her fragile George. She sings as though serenading a child, and her sweet notes float through the paper-thin walls and then down through the wooden floors, and while one might have ordinarily regarded this as some kind of disturbance, Mother and I just sit and listen, transfixed by the beauty of Aida's waiflike voice. The next morning, after breakfast, Aida wraps George in a blanket and props him up on a chair with a pad and a pen set neatly before him. A newspaper has commissioned George to write the story of his life, and despite his increasing frailty, George's pen seems to have found wings. For short periods of time it flies back and forth across the page making short, spasmodic movements, and then the pen comes to rest and George looks all about himself, suddenly ashamed that he is no longer able to dress a point or two above the height of fashion. And then, as though keen to expel this sad reality from his mind, his pen finds life and begins again to dart across the page.

> Our payroll is about $2,300 a week. Do you know what that means? Take your pencils and figure how many families could be supported comfortably on that. Then look at the talent, the many-sided talent we are employing and encouraging. Add to this what we contribute to maintain the standing of the race in the estimation of the lighter

majority. Now, do you see us in the light of a race institution? That is what we aspire to be, and if we ever attain
our ambition, I earnestly hope and honestly believe that
our children, that are to be, will say a good word in their
day for Bert and me and them.

GEORGE WALKER

George gave his final performance in Louisville, Kentucky, in
February 1909, but George Walker was no longer George Walker.
No amount of business could disguise the fact that the man
onstage with me was a mere shadow of the same man who had
stood by my side for sixteen years. The real George Walker had
left the theatrical stage a long time ago, but at least officially,
Williams and Walker came to an end on that night in Louisville,
Kentucky—a long way from the Barbary Coast, a long way from
Broadway, a long way from Buckingham Palace. Williams and
Walker died onstage in Louisville, Kentucky, in February 1909,
but the public were informed that it would only be a matter of
time before George Walker returned. Aida now donned the special George Walker costume and sang "Bon Bon Buddy," but she
understood the truth. The doctor had explained, albeit in painful
detail.

> General paresis is caused by damage to the brain by the
> syphilis-causing microorganism . . . early symptoms of
> general paresis may include personality changes, memory
> loss, speech defects, tremors, and temporary paralysis.
> Seizures may also occur. As the disease progresses, the
> patient deteriorates both physically and mentally.

For more than an hour I have listened to George talking, but I
have little understanding of what George is attempting to com-

municate. He remembers events that he locates in the wrong place and in the wrong sequence. Chronology appears to be irrelevant to him, and if it does have meaning there seems to be nothing that George can do to straighten things out. Whatever fame I have achieved has been gained in partnership with George Walker, and I feel guilty that this affliction should have fallen on my partner's shoulders for him to bear this burden alone. Some days he appears to possess full recall of who I am, while on other days he simply looks at me as though I am not present. When I move, his cloudy eyes sometimes roll, while at other times they remain locked in a ferocious stare. Aida brings in two glasses and a pitcher of water and some cakes and George recognizes her, but he now appears to be incapable of speech for his tongue is flapping but to no purpose. The sun is weak, and some thin rays spill through the open window casting strange patterns of light and shadow on the uncarpeted sections of the floor, and then something seizes George's attention. In the kitchen I can hear a man talking quietly, as though to himself, and Aida notices my alarm. The doctor, she whispers. The doctor has come to see George, but he is waiting until you have finished your visit. I nod, but Aida ignores me and pours a glass of water, which she hands to her husband. He takes it, but Aida has to gently tip it up to his lips so that he can drink, which he does without spilling any. He seems happy now and he manages to smile at his wife, which appears to lighten her heart. Aida gives him another mouthful of water, which he swallows, and I understand that this is more an attempt to elicit another smile than it is an offering to slake poor George's thirst. I leave them alone and close in the door, and then I ease down the steps and onto the street. I look behind me knowing that George no longer needs me. It is now the turn of the doctor.

The next morning Bert eases out of bed having hardly slept a wink. His wife has been awake for some time and he can hear her banging about downstairs in the kitchen. He rubs his eyes and realizes that he will have to make the decision today, otherwise the rumors and gossip will continue to run riot. Mother enters the bedroom carrying his favorite tray, upon which sits a pot of coffee and the newspaper. She sets the tray down on the bedside table and then stands back and waits for her husband to say something to her, but he chooses to say nothing. He stares beyond her to the door and she finally understands that she should probably leave her husband to his own company. He watches the door, and listens to the click as she pulls it in behind her. In order to preserve the dignity of everybody involved he will have to face up to their situation today.

When my old pal is alright . . . we will be together again.

BERT WILLIAMS, *VARIETY*, MAY 1909

Mr. Williams remembered that no matter what kind of statements he issued to the press the Broadway gossip remained loud, with most observers believing that Williams and Walker were finished. For a moment Mr. Williams paused and he looked at the untouched cup of tea and the piece of cake that his wife had set before me, but he stopped short of urging me to eat and drink. He could see full well that this cub reporter was too excited to do anything that would get in the way of the interview and so, with a knowing smile temporarily brightening his face, he leaned back and blew out a huge cloud of smoke and then released a perfectly formed smoke ring. He remembered that by May 1909 *Bandana Land* was over and he decided to take a risk and return to vaudeville as a solo performer at Keith's Theatre in Boston. The bill included the popular family act the Four Keatons, who were veterans of the east-coast circuit, so it was respectful company. However, it soon became clear to Mr. Williams that he needed more practice as a solo performer for he recalled that he was received with some indifference by the Boston public and he knew that without Mr. Walker he would have to totally rework and sharpen his act. A depressed Mr. Williams left the theater and made his way to a nearby bar, having first ascertained that it was appropriate for him to enter.

When Negroes were allowed in white saloons at all, they were restricted to the end of the bar farthest from the door. Pops ignored this the night he walked into the Adams Hotel bar in Boston, which was conveniently situated, being directly behind Keith's Theatre. Bert Williams, who was again on the bill with us, was standing, as required, far down at the other end.

"Bert," said Pops, "come up here and have a drink with me." Bert looked nervously from one white face at the bar to another, and replied, "Think I better stay down here, Mr. Joe."

"All right," said Pops, picking up his glass, "then I'll have to come down there to you."

BUSTER KEATON

Lying in bed, and staring out of the window at the Massachusetts moon with a light buzzing in his head, he thinks now of Mr. Joe making his point, and the looks on the faces of the men in the bar as their curling tongues licked the foamy beer from their thick mustaches. What kind of a place is this Boston? What kind of a place is this America? His father can't decide whether to stay on in New York or return to California, and he seems to have lost his way, and it occurs to Bert that maybe he should just take his parents back to the Bahamas. Back to a place where his father has always insisted that a man can walk tall and feel the sun on his skin, and a lightness to his step, and be free to raise his family. He thinks of Mr. Joe, and those kids of his. Mr. Joe doesn't suffer any foolishness from them, which means that eventually they'll do just fine, but right now they're struggling. However, he knows that this is not his business. Never any sleep in this Boston. Without his wife. Without George, who he imagines is sitting in New York with Aida to comfort him. When he returns to New York he will go straight to George, even though Aida seems to distrust him. Although he believes that he has done nothing to offend George's wife, he imagines that her dislike of him has its origins in her own fears that she might once again lose George, but this time not to another woman. Back in New York he will visit with his partner and rehearse his solo act. Then he will sit with Mother, and then he will rehearse his new act some more. He has original songs and perhaps his New York audience will appreciate him more than the citizens of this moonlit Boston, Massachusetts.

Three new songs and "Nobody," with a bit of talk worked in between tunes, make up Williams' single speciality. Both songs and talk were highly amusing. Williams was never funnier. "That's Plenty" made a capital opening song. There followed a few minutes of talk adapted from his part of "Skunton" in "Bandana Land." Even without a foil in his partner, George Walker, Williams' stupid darkey was a scream. His second song failed to keep up the fast pace, but he picked up speed with a song about a dispute as to the naming of a baby, Williams' suggestion being something like George Washington, Abraham Lincoln, Booker T., and a lot more, until it was learned that the baby was a girl. The discussion ends when the mother announces Carrie Jones as the name. "Nobody" served admirably as an encore, and Williams had to repeat his inimitable "loose dance" several times before they would let him go.

Aida tells me that my husband must be having a gay old time up there on stage by himself, milking all the applause, never a thought in his head for poor George, never a mention of him in his newspaper interviews and articles. But somewhere inside of her she knows that this is false. My husband is the type of man who has respect for everybody, and he carries a deep love for his partner. George does not truly understand what is going on about him, but Aida says that he is hurt. She claims that she can see it in his eyes. An embittered Aida snaps that it is bad enough George knowing that he is not out there onstage with Bert, but to hear that his partner is having a fine time without him is paining her husband's soul. Aida says she *knows* that this is how poor George feels, even though George has not actually said anything to her. The truth is George has not actually said anything to anybody for quite some time.

In July 1909, the *New York Age* announced the unthinkable. The Williams and Walker Company, having *temporarily* lost Mr. Walker to illness, had apparently now lost Mrs. Aida Walker. Mr. Williams sighed deeply as he recalled Aida's less than harmonious departure.

> According to the press reports, Mrs. Walker and the management had not been able to agree on several items in her contract. However, it was evident to everybody that this was only half the story.

My George tried all his life to maintain some dignity and I'm not about to let him down. Not at this stage of his life, when he needs my help. I don't see none of his gentleman friends around here paying him no attention, now that he isn't fun-loving, happy-go-lucky, champagne-drinking, cigar-smoking George. My George isn't a saint, and in his time he's done me wrong and hurt me like all men seem to feel it's their God-given right to hurt a woman who loves them. Don't make no sense, we know that, but some-times men don't make sense. But look at George now. Things are not sitting too well with my George, but he ain't complaining, he's just doing his best to get to the next day with a little dignity, and I'm doing my best to help him. Bert is sending over money, and he's being fair in this respect, but there's something about the way in which he's polishing up his career that doesn't sit right with me, so I say let him be the famous Negro headliner if that's what he wants to be. I'm happy to let him have his name in lights, happy to let him be the biggest colored star in America, and I will stay here and look after my George, who, Bert aside, nobody else chooses to visit. Rumor has it that Bert's new show, *Mr. Lode of Koal,* is nearly ready to open, but who ever thinks about George Walker anymore? George Walker? Why that man's just fallen clean off the map. No Frogs meetings, no Marshall's, no theater, no gallivanting around, just George and myself in 107 West 132nd Street keeping each other company. Just George and myself, and nobody else.

Every morning I wake up and stare at my George and I want to cry. At sunrise I watch him open his eyes like a newborn infant.

Why should a man suffer the indignity of beginning to drift over to the other side when all else about him still seems fine and whole? The doctor says he should go to a sanitarium, where they can take proper care of him and give him treatments, whatever the hell that might mean, but the problem is the doctor doesn't seem to understand that this is George Walker, not some half-drunk, gone crazy, low-billing comedian. This is George Walker facing another day locked up in the prison of himself. My George isn't going anywhere. His career isn't going anywhere. I know this new day that's just broken must look better for Bert, and I just wish I could find it in my being to be happy for him.

During the nights George sometimes finds it difficult to breathe. I don't get much sleep for I have to make sure that everything is comfortable for my husband, and I often try and transfer warmth into his body by pushing up tight against him and this way I can at least feel as though I am passing back some of my own life into him. In the morning I strip off his clothes and gently bathe him, and then I towel him dry, delicately dabbing the droplets of water from his skin. He stares at me as though begging me to explain just what is happening to him.

In August 1909, Mr. Williams's new production, *Mr. Lode of Koal*, was announced, a show over which Mr. Williams was to have equal shares and "exclusive control of the stage management" of the play together with an unreliable producer called F. Ray Comstock. A suddenly animated Mr. Williams recalled that from the beginning this Mr. Comstock seemed to have some financial and communication difficulties, and as a result the rehearsal period turned out to be one of great stress for everybody concerned, particularly Mr. Williams, who, already a prodigious consumer, admitted that he sought solace by drinking and smoking even more than usual.

Even though the old contract had not yet expired . . . I would agree [to Mr. Bert Williams's demands] that in case the said George W. Walker became well again, that he could come into the play and could take part in the contract as though he were a party thereto.

F. RAY COMSTOCK, 1909

People tell me that in his new show, Bert takes out time to poke fun at my Salome dance in *Bandana Land*, but I don't believe Bert would do something like this. Especially not with George ailing so badly. Bert would never put "comic business" before decency and respect.

Bert Williams dances that Williams comedy dance as only Bert Williams can dance it. He danced with three or four girls looking for Hoola. All girls are veiled. . . . Big Smoke unveils the last girl he dances with and finds to his disgust that it is a *man*.

INDIANAPOLIS FREEMAN

Mr. Lode of Koal finally opened in New York on November 1st, 1909, at a theatre on Columbus Circle. The truth is, this was not the most prestigious of New York's theatres, and it was not even on Broadway, but it mattered little. The show lasted for only a very poor forty performances, the highlight being, for Mr. Williams, the surprise thirty-fifth birthday party that the cast held for him, his birthday being on November 12th. He confessed to me that it genuinely shocked him that anybody even knew his birthday, let alone remembered to celebrate it, but the fact was his mind was elsewhere. For some weeks now he had been secretly coughing up blood into his handkerchiefs and hiding them from everybody except his doctor, to whom he admitted that his lungs felt as though they were filled with tar.

The members of the company surprised him by making a number of birthday presents; the female members giving him a gold-headed umbrella and the men a beautiful vase. Refreshments were served on the stage, and several short presentation speeches were made; the comedian replying by saying, "Believe me, I highly appreciate the consideration you have shown, but as I am no speaker, I will close, for that's a plenty."

NEW YORK AGE

If I can't talk to my Bert, and if my own son can't talk to me, then maybe it's time to go home. Maybe it's time to leave my son in the fast grip of this country to which he appears to have mortgaged his soul, and head home. When the boy's mother comes back from California I'll maybe put this to her as a suggestion.

Every week he sends my husband a part of his money, and he still comes to visit. He sits quietly with George, but I can see it in Bert's big mournful eyes that we are losing him to something else. All of us, not just George and myself, all of us are losing slow-moving, slow-drawling Bert. It's in his eyes.

I could see that Mr. Williams was growing tired, and I knew that soon I would have to leave. Most of the newspaper reports of this period summarized Mr. Williams as a great American comedian, but of only one style of work. That of an old-time darky, with his *humor* divided into three easily identifiable classes: grotesque dancing; an original method of walking; and droll voice-work. Listening to his quiet accent, and witnessing his gentlemanly manners, I couldn't help but wonder just how American Mr. Williams felt.

BELIEVE ME

From *Mr. Lode of Koal*

But believe me, I'm getting tired of always
    being de dab
Days worked on me so faithfully
'Til I'se wore most to a rub
You all have heard about dat straw
That broke de camel's back
Well a bubble added to my load
Would shelly make mine crack
But believe me.

A question being asked by many is whether George Walker . . . is greatly missed. . . . When Bert Williams made his initial appearance in the first act, the writer at once thought of Walker, as he had been seeing the two make their first appearance together for years. But the writers [of the new show] have so constructed the piece that as the moments fly, Bert Williams . . . proves that he is capable of starring alone successfully.

As he leaves I want to ask Bert to please stay away and not cause my husband so much distress. Not cause us all so much distress, looking at us with his charity eyes. But I say nothing. It is sometimes difficult to decide which of the two of them is in greater pain.

That last night on stage I was lost, but I hope that people will forgive me. At times I made some sense, but at other moments I watched the rest of the cast watching me and I knew that they were baffled. But now I am gone. Out of sight. On my way back to Lawrence, Kansas, a place I hardly remember for I left there as a young boy and suffered endless humiliations on my way to the west coast. In California I nearly starved to death in the streets, singing and dancing and begging people for money, and then I stole a banjo. The face of the man I took it from is a sleeping face. Did I really steal a banjo from a sleeping man? But I could play the instrument, and owning a banjo made it easier to loiter on the street corners and try to earn pennies from passersby who felt sorry for me. Easier than it was to beg the managers of the various theaters for work. All the way from Kansas and I had been reduced to a banjo-stealing, banjo-playing beggar. I know full well that what I did was wrong. I should ask Aida to find this man, and we should buy him a silver banjo to express our gratitude. Does he know that it was George Walker who survived because of *his* banjo? I will talk to Aida of the banjo.

Aida, why do you sit looking at me so? When I talk to you of the banjo that I found on the streets of San Francisco do you understand what it is that I am talking about? I can see that you are trying to follow my words, but it is difficult for you, isn't it? What do you want from me? A confession that I truly did taste every woman that crossed my path? That I suffer from a touch of Jack Johnson fever? I am no saint, Aida. I lived my life recklessly and I know that being reduced to this state is part of the price that I am paying. Forgive me my weaknesses, and forgive me if I hurt you. That is all I can ask of you, dear wife. Sit here with me in the darkness as I journey back to my hometown of Lawrence, Kansas, by way of the streets of San Francisco. I am not ashamed of where I am from. Sit here with me while I return to my childhood in Kansas territory.

Sometimes I wake up in the morning and the bedclothes are somewhat tousled and things are not as they should be, but always my wife is lying next to me, keeping me warm. Dawn is painful. Lying in bed and staring at the ceiling, watching light bleed slowly across it, watching the day reach out and paint this small room a brighter hue. From ceiling to floor a new day has arrived, but without help I cannot rise to meet it. I never hear about her anymore, and there is nobody I might ask. Does she remember? I imagine that she is still scandalizing the New York theater world and a weak smile creases my lips, but the smile does not have the strength to travel across my face, and the greater portion of the smile remains lodged in my heart.

Mr. Comstock decides to close the show, but it is the theater manager who informs me. Mr. Comstock has not the courage or the decency to approach me directly with this sad news, and I therefore have to give this regrettable information to my company. They are devastated, but I have little choice but to agree with Comstock and attempt to recoup some of my losses. The newspapers are terse with their reporting. "*Mr. Lode of Koal* closes early in New York, and early on the road." I am left with a mass of obligations, and no money, and a mountain of debts that will take me at least one successful season to pay off. Reluctantly, I make my arrangements to return to vaudeville.

My husband cannot properly manage his company business without the help of George Walker. In the past he entrusted much of Williams and Walker's affairs to his partner, and now, without George, he is in disrepair, a plight that distresses him for it suggests a lack of decorum. But what can he do? He must at least try to be responsible, but it is written on his face that this situation is an intolerable burden and he is drinking and smoking and coughing more than ever.

> Mr. Williams told me that for over a week he carried about a contract to play [over] the Moss Stoll circuit abroad at a salary of $1,000 a week; the contract called for four consecutive weeks, with an option to increase the time to twenty weeks, if agreeable to all concerned. All Mr. Williams had to do was attach his signature to the contract and take passage for London, where he would open in one of the big variety halls.

The contract arrived a week ago, but I have no desire to return to England. Not without George. In fact, without George I have no desire.

The beer and whiskey stand before him, large and small, sweet and sour, and he sips one and then the other, and then leans back and closes his eyes for he is suffering bad weather in his mind. Mr. Florenz Ziegfeld has made him a generous offer that will solve many things, but Bert knows that it will also mean trouble. A lawsuit from Comstock, who still imagines him to be under contract, and then the hostile attitude of the white players in the

Follies company. He will, of course, also have to contend with the disappointment of his own people, who will not take kindly to his abandoning the world of colored theater. He opens his eyes and notices a layer of dust on the old bottles that stand behind the bar. He is fully aware of the low regard in which a minority of colored people hold him. Since Jack Johnson became the heavyweight champion of the world, race pride has been rising everywhere, and these days some Negroes look askance at him. It is difficult being Bert Williams today, and because he has an offer from Florenz Ziegfeld there are those who will think that everything must be fine and dandy for him. They will assume that he cannot possibly have a care in the world, but colored show business is at a low ebb, and he knows that at the moment it is better to join a large white show than to star in a colored troupe, particularly so as he is now attempting to work without the business brain of George Walker. Mr. Ziegfeld offered him a leathery hand to shake and seal the deal and ensure that he joins a cast of 125 as the only Negro, supported by an orchestra of forty-two, with sixty Follies girls, and the opportunity to play small parts in a variety of sketches to an extremely well heeled audience. For his initial season in the Follies of 1910, Mr. Ziegfeld will bill him as "The Blackbird with Songs." He drinks his beer. His critics, white and colored, should try making capital humor out of one day in his shoes. He takes a cautious sip of his whiskey, then tips it up and drains the glass. They should try spending one day in his shoes, but he is not complaining. He knows that he does not have the right to complain.

At the darkest point of the night a shadow of fear passes momentarily across his face and he begins to pray furiously to a God that he does not believe in for he can see the door now, and for the first time he notices that it is slightly ajar and voices from the other

side are calling and asking him to come home, begging him to rub
sleep from his eyes and walk in only the shorts that he is wearing,
and on the soles of his feet that are thick and hard, like baked clay,
from years of dancing, pleading with him to move now beyond
the rush of memories that have been cruelly sharpened by time so
that images tumble one on top of the other, seeing the beautiful
curve of Eva's spine as she sleeps, his lover as hot as a two-dollar
pistol, a woman who greets the day like an octopus declaring that
she needs her a "do-right" man but still she refuses to be tongue-
kissed by George or any other man, and Bert asking him, "You
still sweet on her?" as though he has any control over the matter.
"George, you still sweet on her?" And on the other side of the
door is death's thicket of trees that he will soon plunge into, and
the medley of voices soft like summer rain urging him to come
home, come home to Kansas, and George praying furiously to a
God that he doesn't believe in to give him guidance even as he
high-steps his unsteady way toward the door and stutters in a
rough and lisping voice, "Farewell," and again, "Farewell," knowing that soon he will be accompanied on this first part of his
journey.

If George could see him in this blackbird costume he would most
likely refrain from making any statement that related to his
friend's condition, but his opinion would be evident from his
demeanor. Now it is too late. In his final months poor George
could not even recognize his friend and partner. Death scratched
at George's door for a long time before finally easing it open, lur-
ing George through and then escorting him away to another
place. Before George's final emptiness, Bert remembered long
hours spent with George in silence, his partner moving in and out
of lucidity, incapable of recognizing him one moment, and the
next unleashing a torrent of conversation that overpowered him

with its intensity and clarity. At such moments he liked to imagine that maybe everything would eventually be all right with his partner, but then, as suddenly as it had begun, the flood of conversation would end and silence would fall between them like an iron sheet. And this new silence was always more painful than the original silence, for he had not only briefly glimpsed what he now fully understood to be lost, but he had deceived himself. And then Aida would enter the room and barely acknowledge him as she moved toward George, whose eyes always lit up on seeing his wife. Standing deliberately between Bert and her husband she would stroke George's hair and speak softly to him, before turning and leaving again without saying anything to her husband's partner. After Aida's departure he would continue to sit and keep George company in the hope that there might be another outburst of conversation, and then the scratching ceased, and death eased open the door and George passed through and was escorted to another place. It was not unexpected, but death arrived hastily and it was Mother who entered Metheney's Bar and discovered Bert sitting at his small table in the far corner of the badly illuminated establishment. For a moment the patrons all looked up in astonishment, for this finely dressed lady who carried herself with pride was not what they were used to. However, as she looked around, and then began to move toward her husband, they understood and lowered their heads. He looked up at her, but there was no need for her to say anything for he had already guessed what news had brought her into his sanctuary. "George?" His wife nodded and dropped her delicate hand onto her husband's shoulder, but he ignored her and slowly raised his glass to his parted lips and took another drink. Mother turned and left him alone, but before she had even passed out of Metheney's, Clyde D had moved around from behind the bar and refilled Mr. Williams's glass. Bert lifted the now full tumbler of whiskey to his lips, feeling a sudden lethargy as he did so. He could sense it in his blood that some part of his life had just veered off track, and he knew that things would never again be the same. Without George he could look forward to some hard sledding. Solo sledding. Eighteen years with Mr. George Walker as his partner had left him woefully unprepared for life as a single with, or without, a blackbird costume.

Act Three

(1911–1922)

He stares helplessly at the audience as though peering at them through a pane of sharply frosted glass. He can see that out there in the auditorium it is winter, and he feels sure that it must be bitterly cold. He listens carefully to the howling wind, and he knows that night will soon fall. Here, onstage, he shivers for the imaginary window is badly fitted and a gale rattles the frame. He lifts a white-gloved hand to his face and blocks the dazzling light from his eyes, and then he reaches with his other hand, also gloved, and clasps the collar of his threadbare jacket and pulls the material tight around his exposed neck. Who are these people who are staring at this lonely Negro in the window? Clearly they recognize him. However, the bemused looks on their faces suggest that they also feel pity for him, but who are they? It is winter in America. Two bright triangular cones of light cut through the darkness above these people's heads. He looks up and sees the frantic movement of particles that dance like insects, small microscopic objects that swirl and eddy in the bright light.

In the midst of the chilly silence this furious activity fascinates him, and he finds it difficult to tear his eyes from this drama. And then he sees his own reflection suspended in the window; a tall disheveled man stares back at him, one gloved hand to his face, the other to his collar, and he sees the true misery of his own condition and shame strikes him a quick hard blow. But this will be the last time, for never again will he be called upon to stand on the stage of the New Amsterdam Theatre and look out at these eighteen hundred fun-seeking society people. Mr. Ziegfeld has tried to persuade him otherwise, but Ziggy has finally accepted his colored star's decision and informed the always eager press, who have in turn told the world. Next year's offering, the Follies of 1920, will not be graced with the comic bonus of an awkward Negro entertainer who is so clumsy that he cannot walk without dragging his heavy feet; the Follies of 1920 will be deprived of a Negro whose speech is such that it appears that he possesses only the most rudimentary grasp of the English language. Sadly, there will be no colored fool who is so stupid that even the most ignorant among the audience seated in the orchestra stalls will not be able to both pity him and feel superior to him. The Follies of 1920 will be an altogether different entertainment and he feels relief, for it is time to step back and away from his own reflection and save himself. As the wind outside howls he composes himself. The ripple of applause begins to cloud and then rise, and he screws up his eyes and sees that those in the orchestra stalls, and those few in the balcony whose complexions resemble his own, are stirring themselves and climbing to their feet. He bends formally, from the waist, but he keeps his eyes focused on the shower of dancing particles in the two bright cones of light that bully their way through the darkness. Never still, always moving, unable to find peace, their dizzying itinerance fascinates him. Unbending himself at the waist, he stands tall and looks out at the audience, and then he bows again knowing that after nine years his time with Ziggy's Follies is finally at an end. However, he understands that in this theater there will always be motion and unrest in these cones of light, and even after he is gone from this place there will remain some form of silent activity that will always mirror the disquieted movement of his heart with particles leaping first one way, and then the next, invisible to these people's eyes, yet dancing just above their heads. He listens until he can endure no more of the ill wind, or the storm of their approval, and he begins now to wave one gloved hand in their direction and move backward, his eyes all the while focused on his wintry view and the swirling tempest of floodlit activity. Never again will he stand on the stage of "the house beautiful" and look out through this particular window. The journey is over, and all that remains is for him now to seek a place of shelter.

With a single turn of the oversized key he unlocks the dressing room door and slumps down onto the wooden chair. There is no name on the door, only a dull yellow star, but they know to leave him alone if the door is pushed to, which it nearly always is. He dabs the white towel in the china bowl of lukewarm water that the stage manager has placed on his dresser, and he then proceeds to rub his face, discoloring the towel as he does so. There is no need for him to look in the mirror. Only when he is sure that most of the cork has been removed does he stand and peel away his jacket, kick off the oversized shoes, and then collapse back down onto the uncomfortable chair. At forty-four he can feel an ominous fatigue in the deadweight of his body.

The knock on the door startles him. He waits patiently for another knock, or voice, but there is nothing. Eventually, he rises from his chair and moves toward the door, which he opens on Mr.

Ziegfeld, who stands by himself. "I'm sorry, Bert," he begins, "but perhaps you might care to join us in the Circle Bar as we'd like to raise a glass to you." Mr. Ziegfeld does not say who the "we" are that he is referring to, but Bert imagines that Mr. Ziegfeld means his business friends and colleagues, and so he slowly nods ("Thank you") and after his boss has turned smartly on his heels he closes in the door. There is a debt of gratitude to be paid to this man who fought against convention, and many of his established stars, in order that he might include Bert in the Follies of 1910 as the first colored man to appear onstage with the most important performers in the country. Those who had any objection to appearing with a colored man were invited by Mr. Ziegfeld to join another company, but all the members of the Follies company promptly discovered that they did not, after all, have any difficulty playing alongside a colored man, and so Bert found himself onstage and staring out at Mr. Ziegfeld's audience, sometimes singing, sometimes dancing, sometimes telling an anecdote, but always the only tanned player among the Irish, and the Australians, and the Jews, and the Germans, and the Italians, who were the constituent parts in Ziegfeld's new and conspicuously lavish entertainment. In 1910 his nigger face shocked Ziegfeld's patrons with its elastic elegance, while his colored body made them laugh with its alarming, but perfectly choreographed, eccentric grace. And now the Follies of 1919 has reached its conclusion, and Mr. Ziegfeld has asked to see him. He takes the soiled towel and once again rubs it anxiously against his face, and he reminds himself that not all journeys leave footprints that are visible to others. He cannot expect the man who has summoned him to the Circle Bar to know from where he has come or to where he is going. His journey, with all its difficulties, is nobody's business but his own. The continual sucking of his shoes into a muddy path, and the supreme effort that it has taken to consistently dislodge his feet and keep moving on his way, makes him admirable to nobody. After nine years Mr. Ziegfeld and his fellow players see nothing, only the image of a somewhat reticent and grateful man that they wish to see. He puts down the towel and stares unhappily into the mirror, conscious that too much life has flown from this one body in too short a space of time. A pulse still beats within him, that much he is sure of, but the rhythm is weaker now. Death's wings are brushing close by and their touch occasionally startles him, and of late the heaviness of his body has begun to convince him that he may have already entered the final season of his life. He stands and proceeds to change into his street clothes. As he does so his eyes scan the desolate and uncluttered dressing room and they eventually alight upon the solitary whiskey bottle and tumbler.

Up in the Circle Bar the whole cast and crew are gathered around Mr. Ziegfeld, and as Bert enters the room they applaud enthusiastically. He smiles and takes the glass of champagne that is presented to him on a silver tray, and he listens now as Mr. Ziegfeld lists the colored man's achievements and then offers a generous toast, gently tipping his glass in Bert's direction as he reaches his conclusion. There are cheers and all eyes are upon him, for Bert is not only a member of the cast, he is their unacknowledged leader and a beaming Ziegfeld has, from the beginning, suspected that this would be the case. But Mr. Ziegfeld, with his raised glass, still knows nothing of the nature of this colored man's journey. Mr. Ziegfeld does not understand the place that Bert Williams has arrived at today.

> I liked the man as well as any man I ever met and better than most men, for he had so many fine qualities. I admired him as an artist tremendously because he was a

great artist. In fact, he was so great that it was impossible for him to do anything badly. He played down-and-out boarders, porters, cabdrivers, crap shooters, poker players. Any role that called for the downtrodden was Williams's meat. He was a consummate artist in a sea of banality; technically perfect, timing immaculate, his portrayal of his people the only flaw on his otherwise perfect diamond.

FLORENZ ZIEGFELD

And then Miss Fanny Brice edges her way around to greet him personally, as he knew she would, with an already empty champagne glass in her hand and a broad smile on her face, and her eyebrows plucked neatly into the familiar dark arches. To begin with she was one of those who would have preferred that Mr. Ziegfeld not employ a colored man, even if that colored man happened to be Mr. Bert Williams, but she quickly grew to admire his manners and his modesty, and she came to understand that of all the techniques on display on Ziegfeld's stage, his was the one from which she might learn. So, Mr. Williams, you ready to tell me what's next for you, or you planning on keeping a poor girl guessing? She touches glasses with him and then threads her arm through his and leans softly against the stiff formality of his body. Well, well, well, Mr. Williams, has your silvery tongue left that noble head of yours? Here, in the private space of the theater, he finds it possible to tolerate Fanny's behavior, but he knows that beyond the Circle Bar this degree of intimacy is not befitting. But she too understands this, and despite her bluster and bravado, and her origins in burlesque, this is a woman who knows the meaning of the word "decorum." But he cannot tell her what next, for as yet he has no plans, except to sit out the rest of 1919. He says nothing to Miss Fanny Brice and he simply casts her that warm smile of his that he knows makes most folks feel easy around him.

His carefully constructed smile never fooled Eva, who knew full well that he did not approve of her antics either on- or offstage. This being the case, it surprised him that a few months after George's passing, Eva should approach him in the wings of the theater as he was leaving the stage of the Follies of 1911. He was embarrassed that he was still in his makeup, but he could see in Eva's eyes that she was desperate to talk and her unkempt hair, and sunken cheeks, and bare legs suggested that all was not well with George's friend. It was already something of a humiliation for her to sneak into the theater in this manner, for people knew full well who she was, but he nevertheless had no choice but to ask her to wait in the crowded corridor outside his dressing room until he had removed his face. Her eyes began to dart like mice, and he could see that she was disconcerted by his request, but this was too private a process for him to undertake with an audience and he assured her that he would be lively. Eventually he opened the door, begrimed towel in hand, and Eva passed into his dressing room, but he chose not to fully close in the door behind her. For a few moments they sat and faced each other in silence, and then he broke the tension and told her that as far as he was able to ascertain, George had passed on peacefully. He told her that while life had not been easy for George at the end, Aida had made him as comfortable as possible. He noticed Eva flinch at the mention of Aida's name, and he watched as George's friend lowered her eyes. For a few moments she appeared to be deep in thought, and then she looked up and the words came tumbling out. There was a child, nearly three years ago, but I didn't tell George, I just found out where to get myself fixed and I got rid of it as I didn't see how it was going to help anybody. Eva now had

Bert's full attention, but once again she paused and lowered her eyes as though encouraging him to ask a question, or make a statement, but he could think of nothing that he might immediately say and so he remained silent. They sat together for what seemed like an age until Eva abruptly climbed to her feet and forced a smile. I just thought that you should know. He watched as a dejected Eva turned and, with a barely perceptible movement of her hips, left his dressing room and closed in the door behind her.

Fanny Brice squeezes his arm. You ready to go now, Bert? Fanny knows her fellow performer well. He has taken just two sips of his champagne, for this is not his drink of choice. Maybe you should just say something to Ziggy, then I reckon you can be on your way, don't you? He looks over, but Mr. Ziegfeld is surrounded by a press of people and he understands that should he approach he will merely elicit from these men a few conversational volleys before they return to their *real* business. He decides instead to gracefully retreat into the evening. Tomorrow he will compose a letter to Mr. Ziegfeld thanking him for his generosity and support over the years, but right now he will quietly collect a few things from his dressing room and slip through the stage door of the New Amsterdam Theatre for the final time.

He decides to walk back a part of the way home, and as he sets out in the direction of the park he remembers the group of affluent colored men who some years ago, shortly after he began to perform for Mr. Ziegfeld, requested an audience with him. He was familiar with the name of only one of the three men who signed the elegantly worded request, and although he could not be exactly sure why they wished to visit with him, he imagined that it most likely related to potential investment in his future productions. He wrote back and invited them to present themselves at 2309 Seventh Avenue the Sunday after next, and he asked his wife to prepare tea. However, when Mother opened the door on the appointed Sunday afternoon, instead of the three men that she was expecting there were, standing before her, six finely dressed colored men, who she politely ushered into the library, where her husband was waiting. There were not enough chairs to accommodate them all, and so his wife went to find more, and once everybody was settled, and once Mother had poured tea for the men, she left her husband alone with his delegation. Mr. Charles Wilson, a prominent banker, began first, speaking at some length about the importance of Bert to the Negro community, and generally laying the groundwork for what was to come. But by now Bert already knew what was to come, yet he listened patiently, and when their conversation finally corroded into admonition *(Why, Mr. Williams, do you choose to play the shambling, pathetic dupe?)*, albeit carefully dealt, he sat forward and began to speak in a low voice, the words falling softly from his mouth. The Negro I portray is not any man in this room so there is no need for any among you to behave defensively. In fact, I have to believe that my public is sophisticated enough to understand that I am impersonating a particular type who does not exist except in my imagination. Mr. Nail interrupted: And in their imagination, Mr. Williams. We exist in *their* imagination as you portray us, and you reinforce their low judgment of us as dull and pitiable. An exasperated Bert opened his arms wide. Am I responsible for the coarse imagination of some few among my audience? Am I responsible for how the Negro is viewed in America? I am an entertainer, what would you have me do? Stop performing? At this point everyone began to speak at once, assuring him no, of course not. He must not abandon the American stage. Mr. Williams, said Mr. Nail, his voice soaring now above

the others, I would, first, have you perform in theaters that neither bar nor Jim Crow Negroes, and second, I would have you
perform in the guise of somebody whose persona and demeanor
is closer to that of the new, twentieth-century Negro, as opposed
to a low type who is a deliberate travesty of our race. We do not
know, and have never known, this *man* who you impersonate.
Right now we need colored thespians who are prepared to drag
your troubled profession toward dignity, for it would appear that
the Negro is only acceptable on the American stage as long as he
is singing idle coon songs and dancing foolishly. In other words,
as long as he is a close approximation to the white man's *idea* of a
nigger. Players who indulge in this so-called art are wounding the
race, and we are here today to implore you to risk offending your
white admirers by simply casting aside this nigger coon for such
an impersonation has long been out of respectable commission.
Mr. Nail paused before concluding. We sincerely believe that a
man of your talent is fitted for higher things than singing idle
coon songs and dancing foolishly, and surely you must believe so
too. Silence fell in the room and Bert felt resentment begin to rise
like sap inside of him. He looked from one well-groomed colored
face to another, unable to comprehend why these six supposedly
intelligent men could not understand that he was merely playing
a character. His darky was clearly not representative of them or
their worlds. His coon was a very particular American coon as
seen by a man from the outside. In the end, his frustration was
such that he knew he could no longer find any polished words or
phrases to share with these six gentlemen and so he remained
silent and simply let his feverish thoughts run loose in his mind.
Gentlemen, be fair. I am merely trying to give this low-bred colored man some humanity. My colored man may be interpreted by
some as a gin-guzzling, crap-shooting, chicken-stealing, no-good
nigger, but there is more to him than this. He suffers. Our com-
passion goes out to him. He shuffles a little, and he may be slow-

witted, but we surely recognize this poor man. The essence of my performance is that we know and sympathize with this unfortunate creature. Eventually his feverish thoughts stopped racing around his mind, but he could still find no polished words or phrases to share with this delegation, and so he calmly finished his tea and looked from one handsome face to the next.

Shortly after the unsolicited visit of the colored gentlemen, and after his anger at their intrusion into his life had begun to recede, he decided to attempt to repair his relationship with Aida, who seemed to hold him personally responsible for not keeping poor George's name in lights. He sat at the desk in his library and stared at the blank piece of paper before him. A letter seemed like a polite and convenient way to unburden himself, and he fully intended to speak freely about the many issues that seemed to have come between himself and Aida over the years. But his pen would not move. He listened intently to the silence that dominated the house, a silence that was broken only by the noise of automobilists in the street. What was he supposed to say to Aida? That he was sorry that she seemed to have decided to cut off relations with both himself and his wife? Confess to her that her behavior cast a shadow over his memories of the man with whom he had spent the greater part of his working life? He stared at the blank sheet and realized that he could neither ask nor demand anything of Aida, yet to simply unburden himself of his own private hurt seemed an uncharitable gesture. He waited and hoped that by some strange process the right words might come to him, but as the daylight began to fade he found himself looking at the still untouched piece of paper. And then he decided that it might be more appropriate if he were to make the conciliatory gesture of attending an Aida Overton Walker performance and visiting with her after the show, and in this way rekindling what had once been, if not a friendship, a harmonious professional acquaintance.

He also hoped that some of the words that he wished to set down on paper might flow more easily once they were facing each other.

He sits in the front row of the balcony and observes that she still dances well, if somewhat eccentrically and in bare feet, but he understands that this *style* is her own contribution to the world of dance. She moves with some elegance, but to his eyes the outlandish grand sweeping of the hands and arms seems to suggest that Aida is more interested in arousing attention than she is in perfecting dance as an art form. The audience is clearly somewhat mystified by what is being presented to them, and at the conclusion of the evening a good number of patrons withhold their applause, although he does not feel it proper that he should participate in this silent protest. And so he applauds enthusiastically, so much so that those around him look in his direction and immediately recognize the source of the excitement. Embarrassed that he has attracted attention to himself, and eager that his presence should not detract in any way from Aida's evening, it occurs to him that he should leave the theater. The next morning he decides to visit with Aida at her apartment on West 132nd Street and offer his congratulations in person, but having purposefully walked the few blocks to Aida's place, and having climbed the steps to the door and sounded the bell, he waits but nobody answers. He now knocks at the door, and then begins to worry that something might have happened to Aida, for she had looked somewhat distracted onstage, but slowly the truth begins to dawn on him. She does not wish to see him. He knocks again, but this time without passion.

Bert enters the park at Fifty-ninth Street and for a moment finds himself overwhelmed with anxiety about Mr. Ziegfeld, who he hopes will not regard his hurried exit from the Circle Bar as being indicative of any displeasure with the situation. He finds a bench that is shaded by the heavy branches of an overhanging tree, and he sits back and draws deep breaths. He understands that a man should not rummage too closely through the early chapters of his life, for no matter how successful he thinks he is, on closer inspection these chapters will always disappoint. However, on this bright moonlit night he is tempted to look back, not just over his years with Mr. Ziegfeld, but back as far as Riverside, California, and beyond. Mercifully, before the pages begin to turn he arrests his mind for he knows that such reflection will only prove to be painful. He closes his eyes and shuts out the low-hanging branches, and he listens to the wind swelling and stripping the trees of their last remaining leaves, and to his surprise he feels tears behind his lids. Sitting alone in the darkness he begins to weep, for he understands that he has foolishly spilled his life and there is nobody he can blame beyond himself.

ZIEGFELD FOLLIES OF 1914

New York Run: June 1 to September 5, 1914; New Amsterdam Theatre

Authors: Book and lyrics by George V. Hobart; additional lyrics by Gene Buck; music by Raymond Hubbell; special numbers by Dave Stamper

Staging: Leon Errol

Principals: Herbert Clifton, Arthur Deagon, Kitty Doner, Leon Errol, Rita Gould, Kay Laurell, May Leslie, George McKay, Louise Meyers, Vera Michelena, Ann Pennington, Gertrude Vanderbilt, Bert Williams, and Ed Wynn

Notable Numbers: Bert Williams sang "Darktown Poker Club," which he followed with a pantomime of a poker game. In the scene, Williams appeared alone on the darkened stage with a small spotlight shining on his head and shoulders. He held his cards close to his face and pantomimed the entire game: the draw, the study of hand, the bets, the suspicious looks, the raise, the call, the disgust of the loser. Williams also appeared as a caddie trying to teach golf to Leon Errol.

The Follies of 1914 toured more extensively than any previous season of the show. He lost count of the number of cities that they visited, and since he was the only colored performer in the production, a new city always presented him with new problems. In Cleveland, Ohio, he read the short column in the local paper. It announced the demise of Aida Overton Walker, but it said nothing about the cause of death. He knew that in the two years that had passed since he had witnessed her eccentric performance, Aida's shows had continued to be much remarked upon, with particular reference to both their increased *originality* and the obviously frail condition that Aida displayed each time she took to the stage. However, he had heard that of late Aida had stopped performing altogether and that she had chosen to retreat from public life. Apparently she seldom ventured out of the apartment on West 132nd Street, and then suddenly Aida was an item in a newspaper in Cleveland, Ohio. Bert sought out Mr. Ziegfeld and explained that he would have to immediately return to New York for a funeral, but Mr. Ziegfeld was aware of the situation and he had already made travel arrangements for his colored star. He assured Bert that he should not worry, for his place on the bill would be adequately covered until he felt able to return.

A forlorn-looking Mother met her husband at Pennsylvania Station and informed him that word had reached her that it might prove to be awkward should either of them attempt to attend Aida's funeral and pay their respects. Apparently the members of her dancing circle remained somewhat biased against the Williamses, and so Mother had decided that they should simply send flowers. As they were being chauffeured from the station back uptown to 135th Street, a confused and somewhat hurt Bert realized that he could live with this decision as long as his wife would let him choose the bouquet. This way he would not feel entirely stupid for having left Cleveland. This way he could at least imagine that he had some role in the proceedings.

> Aida Overton Walker, easily the foremost Afro-American woman stage artist, widow of George Walker of the formerly famous team of Williams and Walker, died Sunday night (Oct. 11) at her home, 107 West 132nd Street, New York. Mrs. Walker had been confined to her bed for about two weeks with an attack of kidney trouble. Her last appearance was at Hammerstein's in *Modern Society Dancers*, August 3rd.
>
> *VARIETY*, OCTOBER 1914

Bert set aside the newspaper and closed his eyes. The *New York Times* insisted that the cause of death was not congestion of the kidneys, as had been widely reported, but a nervous breakdown. Aida Walker was only thirty-four years old, and funeral services were to be conducted by Dr. Bishop of St. Philip's Church, the same man who had married her and George Walker. According to the reporter, rumor had it that Aida Walker left no real estate and only $250 in personal property. Bert opened his eyes and he began to cough violently. The pains in his chest had returned, and once again his lungs felt as though they were filled with tar.

Reaching swiftly into his trouser pocket, he stifled his hacking with a handkerchief for he didn't want Mother to hear him like this.

I knocked on Aida's dressing room door, although I didn't know what I might say to her about the skittish jumping about that I had just beheld. You never could tell with fiery little Aida what kind of a mood you were going to find her in. Since we lost George, Aida had become somewhat crazy both onstage and off for, having nursed him fiercely during his illness, it was as if she was now truly abandoned and free to exhibit herself however she pleased. On the night that I attended her eccentric performance the audience did not know what to make of Aida's antics, but I applauded loudly—too loudly—then made my way backstage to her dressing room and knocked on the door of the woman the newshounds liked to call the "chocolate-hued star." Aida opened the door and stood before me with a bottle dangling from one hand and a cigarette in the other. Her silk gown was yawning a little too much at the neck, and as George's widow began to speak I could smell that she had already been drinking hard from the bottle.

He greeted me with that fake smile like he'd bought it cheap someplace, and I looked him up and down and then threw back my head and laughed out loud. I didn't think it was possible, child, but these days you're looking more than ever like a smoked white man. You coming in, or what? I moved to one side and he passed me by, clearly smelling the liquor as he did so, but no doubt hoping that this meant that there would be no need for him to say anything about the performance that he had just witnessed. I knew full well that he didn't have no respect for my dancing. I pointed. Sit down, sit down, man, or you too high and

mighty to spend time with dark-toned colored folks? He sat and
as I bent to pour him a glass of whiskey my gown parted and I
exposed a breast. I turned suddenly and caught him looking hard
at my body. You think I ain't much better than a dance hall harlot,
is that it? He opened his mouth to speak but I held up a solitary
finger. Hush. You ain't no diamond-decked lover like George, but
you got something down there, don't you? Well, don't you, or is
that why George had to take care of Lottie too? I watched him
and could see something in his stomach fall, but George's thing
for Lottie wasn't news to nobody. Well, what you looking at, Mr.
Corkface? You think George only had a keen eye for a white
ankle, is that it? What's the matter, Mr. Celebrity? You waiting
for the white man to tell you it's okay to take some of this hot
chocolate? Tell me, you ever had a colored girl? For I know you
sure as hell never laid a thing on Lottie, which is why I don't
blame my George for giving the poor woman a little something
to warm her up. I mean, Mr. Williams, just what kind of rusty-
colored gangling man are you anyway? You ever had a woman,
period? Come on, man, don't look at me like that, making that
bottom lip all fat and ugly. Baby, I'm just gonna cock my foot
right here and if you want some of this then you better take that
thing out of your pants and come and get some. Or maybe that
ain't why you've come a-visiting. You come back here to tell me
about my dancing, or to shoot off about the $50,000 a year they
say you're making, or to convince me how it ain't no disgrace to be
colored but it sure can be inconvenient? I mean really, why you say
all that shit to people anyway? You know it ain't right to be talking
so, but it's like you got those damn fool newspapermen playing
you like a tin whistle, making you look dumb and making us look
dumber. Come on, be a man, you came back here for some of this,
ain't it, for I see the way you been looking at me over the years,
Mr. High and Mighty Stage Coon, wondering if George really

did make your woman holler, and wondering what it would be like to take a sweet little piece of George's world. Well come on, nigger, take that long thing out of your pants and show Aida what you got. It's okay, man, I'm ready for you. But even as I tried to coax some heat into him I watched as he began to back away toward the door. Or maybe you don't want to do it here. You want to come by the apartment tomorrow morning? Come knock on my door, Mr. Corkface, and I'll be waiting all hot and ready to take care of you. You come by tomorrow morning, you hear? He nodded quickly as he opened the door, and I listened to the echo of it slamming long after he had passed from view. This damn fool know-it-all West Indian, with his white heart, who deserted our colored stage just when we needed him most. I knew full well that in the morning he would come by and visit with widow Aida, but I wasn't giving nothing up for this white man's fool. Not for his coon ass. I knew he would come by, but I was fixing to make him look foolish for everything he'd already done to me and to George and to all of us. I'd already decided to stand his stupid black ass up in the street and see how he liked to be played.

Sitting by himself beneath the overhanging branches of a tree in a moonlit Central Park, he weeps silently. It is true, journeys don't always leave footprints. His poor father understood this. To-morrow he will write Mr. Ziegfeld a letter and make everything all right. Surely, Mr. Ziegfeld will understand his sudden depar-ture was not meant to suggest any unhappiness or discomfort, and the letter will, of course, contain no mention of anything beyond gratitude.

Her father-in-law's eyes are open and he stares quizzically, as though struggling hard to see something behind her, but Lottie ignores the anxiety in his gaze and reaches down her hand and quietly closes both of his lids. Her mother-in-law sits by the side of the bed, still in her nightdress, clearly shaken with grief and incapable of either speech or action. Lottie touches the older woman's shoulder and tells her that her husband most likely suffered a heart attack in the dead of night, but the older woman says nothing, her mouth simply drooping ajar. Lottie looks again at her father-in-law, and senses that with the arrival of the final blow, relief must have flooded the poor man's body, for he appears to be strangely serene. After the morning in which he cut both Billy "Too Fine" Thomas and the innocent customer, a deeply disturbed Fred Williams never again set foot inside his barbershop, and he and his wife chose instead to move somewhat unpredictably between their son's house, the Harlem residence that Bert had acquired for them, and Riverside, California, as they made laborious preparations for a return to the Bahamas, but neither of them could decide when this migration might occur. Eventually a depressed Fred began to withdraw even further into himself, and the more he did so, the deeper became the melancholy that consumed his desolate wife. But now, as Lottie looks down at this peaceful man, she is overwhelmed with a sense of relief for she is sure that the demons that had begun to haunt his soul have now almost certainly abandoned him. His son is touring somewhere in the midwest with the Follies of 1912 and later this same day, after she has made all the funeral arrangements, she will wire him the news of his father's sudden departure and she will choose her words carefully for she wishes to spare her husband any feelings of guilt or responsibility. Casting a final, baleful glance at the still-warm body, she decides to leave her grieving mother-in-law alone with her late husband, and begin to assiduously apply herself to the tasks at hand. By doing so she is hopeful that she might ensure that her father-in-law is treated expeditiously and that her husband's already troubled spirit is spared the worst of this shock.

He stares at the instrument that scrutinizes him. Only the clicking heartbeat of the machinery lets him know that it is alive and well, but whatever magic occurs inside the black box is beyond his knowledge. Despite his misgivings, he has little choice but to trust that the device will accurately record his offering and not impose its own authority upon him. He already understands that this may be the new art of the twentieth century, a means of transporting one individual performance to all corners of the country, and he wishes to be a part of it. So, when Mr. Tarkington Baker asked him if he might be persuaded to participate in a moving picture he cautiously agreed, and he now finds himself peering at the camera in the hope that this transaction might produce a fair and faithful record. However, the black box promises him nothing and it stares back as though daring him to perform. And so this is now his audience? The instrument gives him no clue as to what is expected and it has occurred to him that he is therefore free to do whatever he pleases. We're ready now, Bert. Mr. Baker has set up the scene, and put the players in position, and all eyes are on Bert. He stares at the black box and a sharp surge of excitement rushes through his body. The box cannot howl in protest. It cannot leave its tripod and walk out in disgust. The box cannot disapprove of him. Everybody ready? Bert? He moves into place in front of the camera and looks from astonished face to astonished face, but nobody says a word. And then he gazes at his audience, who are hidden away somewhere at the back of the black box.

One week later the film is edited and he squats awkwardly in a room that is crowded with people and equipment, so much so that he finds it difficult to secure a space into which he might bend his tall frame into a sitting position. Although it seems unlikely, there are four men in this tiny dark place, and then somebody's hand reaches up and switches off the light and the images begin to flicker against the wall. For eleven minutes he sees himself performing an act that he has never before witnessed, moving easily, the hand gestures perfect, the timing flawless. He watches himself and in the darkness he is quietly moved. And then it is over and the anonymous hand snakes up the wall and snaps the light back on and Bert continues to sit and say nothing even though all eyes are upon him. He pauses for a moment, and then he speaks: *Again*. For a brief moment Mr. Baker looks quizzically at him, and then he simply waves to the man behind the projector and again the room is plunged into darkness and the images begin to flicker against the wall. As the film thunders through the projector for a second time, Bert looks at the moving picture and he feels proud of it, although he already understands that not everybody will share his feelings. When the projection is completed, and the lights are turned back on, he scans the room with a smile upon his face, but it soon becomes apparent that he is the only one who is smiling. Five weeks later they premiere the motion picture at a location in Brooklyn, but he is advised that it might be better for all concerned if he does not attend. And so he waits to hear the news of how his audience have responded to the film, and the single word "riot" floats back to him. They are angry because he has chosen not to cork his face. Why else would they respond like this? Between his needs and his audience's expectations he walks a tightrope, but with only a black box for guidance he now knows that he is always liable to miscalculate. He understands the nature of the problem—he needs to see, hear, feel his audience—but they too must understand that there is, on his part, no desire to cause offense.

Dancing in the Dark

DARKTOWN JUBILEE (1914)

The appearance last night of the celebrated Negro comedian Bert Williams in top hat and zoot suit in the motion picture *Darktown Jubilee* caused a powerful outburst
of resentment among the audience, which could not be
contained without violence breaking out. Although long
used to the vaudeville headliners reaching out to embrace
this new world, audiences have every right to expect
them to remain loyal to the mode of entertainment that
brought them their celebrity on the planks. But not so
with our Mr. Williams. Gone was the familiar "darky
humor" heavily laden with pathos, and in its place he
gave to us an uncorked colored person of cunning and
resourcefulness that left a sour taste in the mouth of all
who had paid money to attend this presentation.

After the third motion picture Bert decides no more and he quietly turns his back on the black box. His final two films (in familiar blackface and gloves) have not been a happy experience, and
he sees little point in persevering with an art form that, entombed
as it is in silence, cannot even offer him the relief of dialect-
drawling humor, or the possibility of conquering the audience
with a plaintive tune. Bert instructs his wife that they no longer
take calls from Mr. Tarkington Baker.

A NATURAL BORN GAMBLER (1916)

Williams gives his watermelon grin most satisfyingly.

FISH (1916)

The colored character is a charming big child of arrested development.

Nineteen eighteen debuts as a hard year, with America still in the war, and winter icy cold, and his wife suffering from large mood swings and feeling that the bloom is permanently off her rose, and Bert choosing to hide away in his library and spend a great deal of his time staring out the window at the colored people who walk confidently up and down Seventh Avenue. Africa is in the air again, and he hears rumors of a small Jamaican man down at 125th Street who is urging colored folks to go back to Africa, where he promises them they will meet black kings and queens, and they will discover a place where they might live in peace at some remove from all the hostility of American life. He and George tackled Africa a long time ago, but does anybody remember their productions? *In Dahomey? Abyssinia?* He suspects not, for the musical seems no longer to be in vogue now that Bob Cole and Ernest Hogan, and George Walker himself, have long since succumbed to the "entertainer's disease." Once upon a time it was said that all over America the Negro was dancing himself to death, but now, during these leaner times, Bert sometimes feels as though he is the only colored man still performing in America, albeit to Mr. Florenz Ziegfeld's audience of white people, and so in 1918 he decides to take time off, having informed Mr. Ziegfeld that he has family business to attend to. Bert spends whole days sitting in his library and letting his mind wander, thinking of purchasing a roadster, or wondering about the wisdom of an airplane excursion, only to have his reverie rudely interrupted by his wife opening or slamming doors, or shouting instructions to the housekeeper. Not wishing to complain, he invests greater periods

of time in Metheney's, where the talk is increasingly related to the
question of whether the colored man should go off and fight the
white man's war, or the folly of the government at Washington, or
the possibility of Jack Johnson regaining his heavyweight crown.
These quiet conversations are always conducted in the spirit of
Metheney's, and although he has opinions on a wide range
of subjects he finds it difficult to enter these fierce, but muted,
debates. An increasingly strident Harlem is changing and, Mother aside, there is nobody to whom he might turn and air his
thoughts, and so he often sits in Metheney's and nurses his drink
and wonders if he did the right thing telling Mr. Ziegfeld that he
would not be taking part in the Follies of 1918 for he wished to
stay home and help his wife, who was suffering from melancholia.
However, it has to be admitted that since Mother has discovered
the curlers and magic pomades of Madame C. J. Walker, and dis-
pensed with her dozens of hats and bonnets, some of her despondency seems to have dissipated. The truth is, no matter how long
he muses over the rights and wrongs of his decision to take time
out from the Follies, he understands that he will never reach a
successful conclusion, and so he resigns himself to simply sitting
in Metheney's and drinking steadily, and listening to conversations that he feels he should not participate in, led by men he
finds it difficult to speak with, about subjects that he feels he
knows too much about. Clyde D pours him yet another drink,
and Bert occasionally lifts his head and watches America turning
in one direction while he remains seated and worried that perhaps
he is incapable of moving forward at either the same pace or in
the same direction as his adopted country. Down in midtown the
beautiful girls, and the lavish costumes, and the elaborate settings
of the Follies of 1918 are being applauded by men and women who
might, after the show, choose to go up and onto the roof of the
New Amsterdam Theatre and join patrons such as Diamond Jim

Brady, or William Randolph Hearst, and savor the late-night antics of Ziggy's intimate rooftop Frolic. Back up in Harlem, Bert Williams is taking a break, but he has already decided that next year, if Mr. Ziegfeld will have him back, he will return to the New Amsterdam Theatre and Mr. Ziegfeld's colored star will rejoin the Follies of 1919.

As he leaves the park bench and begins to walk slowly uptown through Central Park, he remembers that again, tonight, on his final performance with the Follies, he had difficulty seeing them through the frosted glass. He knew that should he reach up his hand and wipe the glass, his confusion would be revealed, and such a move would therefore be humiliating. He has suffered like this for the whole season, and he has survived many fraught moments when he found himself standing on the Follies' stage and looking out at the audience without either fully seeing or hearing them. Luckily, he has had little trouble with the actual performance, which is like a broken-backed shoe into which he can easily step, but whenever he tries to focus on the audience his mind often wanders aimlessly and he discovers that he can no longer communicate. At least the patrons have not noticed, that much he is sure of, but it frustrates him that he can never predict when this affliction might strike. The Follies of 1919 has been a trial, for each evening he has walked onstage consumed with dread, and on this evening, at his farewell performance, he once again found himself staring helplessly at the glass, unsure if the audience could actually see the full terror of the man in the window who has been so unforgivably clumsy with his own life and who is peering out in their direction. Leaving tonight's stage he felt great relief, for he understood that never again would he have to withstand this nerve-racking turmoil of uncertainty, and now, after Mr. Ziegfeld's Circle Bar party, he is content to find himself walking alone through Central Park and in the direction of 135th Street and into retirement in a Harlem that, to his dismay, seems to be increasingly dominated by sporting-house keepers, but a Harlem that nevertheless feels like some kind of home.

In retirement he soon discovers that one unstructured day leads aimlessly to the next, and he rapidly falls into a stupor of illness. His wife worries at his physical and mental state, for he begins to keep strange hours, often alert and awake in the middle of the night, but during the day he dozes long and hard, and he will only pick idly at his food. Finally Lottie can take no more and she decides to call a doctor and plead with him to examine her husband. Exhaustion of mind and body is the young doctor's analysis of the situation, and although his wife finds this prognosis unsatisfactory she pays the man and resolves to nurse her husband back to health. She thinks about writing to his aging mother in California, but she understands that her always private husband may consider this an unwelcome intrusion into his affairs, and so she quickly dismisses this thought. She also puts to one side her hope of one day inviting her three nieces to New York City, for she knows that her husband is not strong enough to endure the confusion. Mr. Ziegfeld, like the rest of the profession, hears the sad news of Bert's post-Follies spiral into drinking and despondency, and he sends a huge bunch of mixed flowers in which roses are the dominant species. There are so many flowers that it is easy for his wife to divide them into four vases, which she places at various points in the house, leaving the largest and most impressive of the bunches in her husband's library. The high odor permeates the whole house, but she cannot decide whether it is a good thing or not to remind her husband of Mr. Ziegfeld at precisely the time that he is trying to move beyond the Follies. However, he enjoys the scent, which lingers even after the flowers have begun to wilt, and he reads his newspaper and stares out the window and tries to obey the doctor's orders to take rest. Viewed from the outside it appears as though the famous colored performer is assiduously following instructions, but inside himself Bert tries to still a pounding heart, and in his mind he wishes to stifle his own private knowledge that he has no plans as to what he might do next. His inability to make a decision of any kind is causing him great embarrassment, and these days when he smiles weakly at his wife, whose lips he remembers taste as sweet as cherries, she often feels like turning away and shedding tears.

The young man holds a small notepad flat in the palm of one outstretched hand, and in the other hand a pen hovers as he looks intently in the direction of a visibly harrowed Bert Williams. Before the young man is a cup and saucer and a teapot, and there is also a small plate upon which sits a piece of cake and a fork, but the man is clearly not interested in either food or drink for he has made the short crosstown pilgrimage for one purpose only, and that is to interview the most famous colored performer in the world for the *New York Post*, and whoever else he might sell the exclusive to. For a whole year he has been writing to Mr. Williams and requesting an interview, and finally he has made a breakthrough for he is now sitting before his hero, whose large physique and courtly manners are precisely what he was expecting. Nineteen eighteen was a good year to begin requesting this interview, largely because the word on Broadway was that Mr. Bert Williams would never again perform, and that his one-year hiatus from the Follies was merely a way of delaying the inevitable announcement of his retirement. Bert did not answer the young man's initial requests, even though he always admired the polite unhurried manner in which the solicitations were framed, but eventually he relented and the colored youngster is now sitting before him, his thick lips strangely misshapen as though he has recently been struck in the mouth, and his borrowed suit hanging loose for it is far too big for his young bones. He can see that the colored youngster is nervous and so he tries to set him at ease with a smile, but it is obvious that nothing short of beginning the actual interview is going to make the young man feel comfortable. The first questions are factual enough, inquiring as to where he was born, and when he came to America, and if he is now an American citizen. Bert confirms that indeed he is now an American citizen. The young man continues and follows the contours of Bert's career up until he joins the Follies, correctly identifying dates, places, productions, and generally winning his subject over with his impressive range of knowledge. But then the young man, perhaps sensing Bert's fatigue, suddenly decides to change gear and open up the interview. He asks Mr. Williams if he feels like a Negro American. This question renders Bert ill at ease and he is unsure how to respond, but the polite young man does not push him on this issue. He turns instead to the nature of the relationship that Mr. Williams enjoyed with Mr. George Walker, and he asks him if it would be true to suggest that his most important work was done in the company of George Walker. Bert pauses before answering, which gives the young man an opening to fire off another question. Of all the things that he has done since Mr. Walker's passing, what, if anything, has given him the greatest pleasure? For a moment Bert is silent as he tries to work out if somewhere, buried beneath this young man's general bonhomie, good humor and ill will aren't lurking side by side. Does the young man believe that he has done no good work since breaking with George nearly ten years ago? In fact, he feels sure that he should not be pressed in this manner to judge his own contribution for surely this is the job of the fellow with the pad and pen. But he decides not to admonish the young reporter and instead he suggests that in the ten years since the demise of Williams and Walker there has been much to be grateful for. Aside from his many stage performances, and the three short films that he starred in, he has perhaps proved himself to be one of America's most successful recording artists. The young man listens and writes assiduously, occasionally nodding as his pen scratches back and forth across the page, but it is too late, for the man's implication is clear; he believes that without George Walker, Mr. Williams has underachieved. A thoroughly disappointed Bert has read and heard it all before. The young reporter looks up and wonders if Mr. Williams is aware that a play called *The Emperor Jones*, written by Mr. Eugene O'Neill, will soon be produced starring the colored actor Charles Gilpin. Bert keeps the smile anchored to his face, but it is the phrase "colored actor" that bothers him, with its unpleasant implication of failure on his part, for he is most certainly not regarded as a colored actor. He is a colored performer. "Actor" is a term that suggests a certain dignity, and it implies a necessary distance between the performer and the character to be interpreted. This one word, "actor," if properly applied to him, might have spared his soul much misery, but he understands that nobody, including this reporter, considers him to be an actor. The young man looks across at him and once again asks the same question, and this time Bert smiles and nods his head. Yes, he is aware of *The Emperor Jones*, and he remembers Charles Gilpin well, for some years earlier the young "actor" had appeared as a chorus singer in *Abyssinia*, whooping it up with the best of them and doing a little dignified buck dancing. Williams and Walker provided Mr. Gilpin with his professional break, for both he and George felt it important to recognize and encourage talent. Clearly some of this is news to the excited young man, but it upsets Bert that Charles Gilpin should now be spoken of in the present and future tense, while the whole tone of the young man's conversation with him speaks to the past tense. Until, that is, the journalist reaches the final question and asks his subject if he can imagine himself forming another company and going out on the road, or did the Follies of 1919 really signal the end of Bert Williams's stage career? He looks closely at the young man and he chooses to simply stir this question into his cup of tea and ignore it. Bert takes a sip of his tea and then discreetly places the cup back into the circle of the saucer before climbing to his feet. The young man also stands, understanding that the interview is now over, but he worries for despite the thin smile on Mr. Williams's face he is concerned that he may have caused some offense to the great Negro performer. Mother enters the room, as though on cue, and the two men shake hands, and then Mother escorts the young man out of the room. Bert sits carefully, his knees twin-pointed hillocks on which he rests his flat palms, and he listens for the door to close. Alone now in his library, the evidence of a meeting before him in the shape of the man's still full cup of tea and his untouched slice of cake, his reputation as a Negro performer under scrutiny, he wonders again about his future.

Clyde D moves slowly. He pours another drink and then pauses as though he wishes to say something, but whatever it is that he wishes to say has momentarily slipped out of his mind. However, he knows better than to hover around Mr. Williams's table, so he turns and moves back to the bar, where he will remain until Mr. Williams's glass once again needs tending. These days the noise from the avenue is loud and it leaks into the place and disturbs the peace of the afternoon. In Metheney's day a man could barely hear a raised voice in the street, but today the competing noises of vendors, automobiles, and streetcars all bully their unapologetic way into Clyde D's bar. It's a new, busier world, but old Mr.

Williams is protected in this bar from both prying eyes and conversation.

He looks again at his newspaper, careful to note anything that is reported from England. He never did return there, but he still tells himself that, despite the tedium of the journey aboard the SS *Aurania*, one day he will make it back to Buckingham Palace where the king and queen welcomed the colored players so graciously for their royal command performance to celebrate the ninth birthday of the young Prince of Wales, Edward. He remembers it was not a warm day, and he worried as to how his company would manage everything in the garden of this English palace that was guarded by soldiers who held their helmets under one arm like severed heads. First a stage had to be built, and then all the costumes and props transferred from Shaftsbury Avenue, which was a mile or so across the center of London, and then all the paraphernalia had to be laid out and made ready for the performance. George was eager to make sure that they were dressed properly, his own gemstones as big as marbles, but the actual details of the performance he left to his partner, and so for most of the morning and afternoon Bert found himself rushing from one place to the next confirming that all members of the company were aware of the significance of this day. Williams and Walker would be setting both colored elegance and colored beauty, and a little of their own "African royalty," before this English king, and by embracing Africa they were breaking the American stranglehold on their lives and engaging with something historically and culturally unique. According to George, they were internationalizing the stereotype, and by doing so hoping to escape its harness, but George was realistic enough to admit that a royal audience might not understand this. Inevitably, when the hour for the performance finally arrived, a fatigued Bert could barely summon the strength to get into his costume, let alone cakewalk back and forth across the makeshift stage. In the end, it transpired that it was the cakewalking that proved most popular, especially with the young Prince Edward, and at the conclusion of the afternoon the prince insisted that an exhausted Bert and George, his favorite coons, give him a private demonstration of the correct cakewalking technique, laying particular emphasis on the sliding and gliding for the boy could already intuit that his young legs were too short to properly high-step. But this was a long time ago, and now George and Aida are gone, and here in this Harlem bar any thoughts of his weary body cakewalking on a makeshift stage in the garden of an English palace seem unimaginable. Perhaps the polite young man who visited him with a notepad and an eager pen already understood what he has not yet admitted to himself. That his days as a performer are at an end, for he suspects that unless he is on the glamorous playbills of Ziegfeld's Follies, few people will relish the opportunity of witnessing old Bert Williams performing *low* comedy in blackface, with shuffling feet, and his raggedy clothes falling from his backside. After all, who wishes to recognize *this* Negro today?

Bert falls into the habit of leaving Clyde D's Bar late at night and wandering the streets of his city on bruised and swollen feet until the sun comes up. He observes the colored citizens of New York going about their night business, and he studies them, he looks at their posture, listens to how they speak to one another in short excitable bursts, and he observes their often flamboyant hand gestures. These days there are many who don't recognize him, including those who have arrived fresh off the trains from the south and who might be familiar with his name, but who certainly don't know his face. The sight of this tall, heavyset, light-skinned man ambling around the streets of Harlem shod in carpet slippers only arouses feelings of pity in the hearts of those who look on. Why is this slow-moving man not home and tucked up safely in a warm bed? What can he be looking for out here on these early-morning streets? As he passes by strangers he smiles at them, for he is a booster for New York and he loves the way the city rises toward the sky, he loves the Brooklyn Bridge, the coal-powered elevated trains, the noise, the dirt, the rivers alive with their multitude of craft; this is his city, and these are his people, and as he walks he imagines that in its perversely detached way New York City understands him, but eventually sleep invades his tired limbs and he finds himself at the top of the short flight of steep steps that lead right up to his door, and he pauses for a moment and then slowly turns around and looks out on a lamplit Seventh Avenue knowing that tonight he has once again beheld the three stages of dawn. First, he witnessed the accidental leak-age of light that hardly altered the darkness. Second, he saw the blackness turn a dark, royal blue. And finally, as he entered his block, he could see green leaf against brown trunk, and he stands now and observes the door handle distinct from the door, and the individual colors of Mother's drapes in the windows, and then the streetlamps blink off and the avenue is now once again illumi-nated by the reliable light of the day, and soon he will be able to ease the slippers from his swollen feet.

When he wakes up he realizes that the sun is shining directly into his face. He levers himself upright on the sofa in the library and he notices that Mother has already placed the daily newspaper in his lap. These days this early-morning exchange represents the true extent of their intimacy, and he feels powerless to improve upon it. He has dreamt that he was back on the road leading a new company that comprised just himself, George, and Aida, and every city they played in they broke box office records. Strangely, he remembers that the audience in the stalls contained only colored folks, while the white people sat upstairs in the balcony and looked on somewhat cautiously. Of course, the most important thing of all was the fact that there was no makeup upon his face. George danced a graceful jig and looked over and smiled at him, and then he woke up and discovered that the sun was shining directly into his face and that his wife had carefully placed the daily newspaper in his lap.

He looks from one face to another eager to ask them why they are staring down at him in this fearful manner. In fact, why are they standing over him? Their mouths are moving but he can hear nothing except the sound of the sea rushing around in his head, rising and falling, the waves lapping gently from one side of his nappy wig to the other. Every face is white. He remembers. His company is all white and they are on the road, at the Garrick Theatre in Detroit, with his new production, *Under the Bamboo Tree*. It is 1922 and Bert has made a comeback. Bert Williams is producer, star, and leader of a new company, but without George this is futile. The box office is weak, and he is sick and incapable of dressing himself, and the door to his mind is ajar, so much so that he seems to have little control over who or what wanders in, but he understands that he must continue for without him there will be no show, yet there is an aspect of horror on the faces of those who look down at him for clearly they see something that has shocked them. He had thought seriously about formally announcing his retirement, but he finally admitted to himself that his short journey from his library to Clyde D's and back again was disrupting his soul, and so after two years his wife was happy when against all expectation he tore up the numerous drafts of his "retirement" press release, and he announced that he would be forming a new company and touring the country with a *tradi-*

tional type of show. However, it quickly became clear, both to his company and to paying audiences, that Bert Williams had under-estimated the pressures of leading a company, and he began to struggle through performances, and sweat cried from his armpits the moment he left the quiet of his dressing room, and his joints jerked to little purpose when he attempted to dance for his whole rig was rusted over, and at the conclusion of each evening he could no longer bow deeply, or smile broadly, or bathe in the lux-ury of applause. Soon his wife was begging him to return home to New York and admit that his body and mind could no longer take this beating, but he decided to persevere, and now, above him, the circle of white faces begins to spin like a child's top and he closes his eyes and the world fades to black. He remembers completing the matinee and so this must be the evening performance. And then he feels the staccato motion of the automobile as it picks its careful way through the dark streets of Detroit. The wind is high and it rocks them first one way and then the next, but he can hear nothing except the sea in his ears. He is cold, and his whole body begins to shiver now as he remembers that it was here in Detroit, twenty-six years ago, in 1896, that he first adopted cork and became somebody else. He laughs for he has yet to take off the same cork. Perhaps this is what they were staring at? The evi-dence of what he has become. A face that was put in place in the last century but that, in this new century, no longer makes much sense to either white or colored. Just who is this corkfaced colored man who claims to be their leader, yet who seems incapable of paying their wages? At the hospital the doctor feels his patient's brow with the back of his hand, and then he takes a towel and wipes the offending makeup from himself. He plucks a watch from his vest and reaches down and lightly touches his patient's wrist with two fingers. He shakes his head and takes a deep intake of breath. No, he says, turning to the company manager. No, this man cannot set foot on a stage again. He gestures to the company manager to move some few paces away, but he does not realize that his patient can hear nothing beyond the rise and fall of the sea that brought him to this country as an eleven-year-old boy on a saltwater voyage that has been both the making and the unmaking of him. Unless you can replace him, begins the doctor, then you must close your show for this man must immediately return to New York City. I take it you know how to contact his kin? And you should instruct the Michigan Railroad Company to send a wheelchair and blankets. The company manager nods and asks the doctor how he might settle the bill. The doctor casts a cursory glance in the direction of his patient and then he shakes his head.

His wife lays him out in their bedroom and she does her best to keep the fire roaring. She understands how important it is that Mr. Williams achieve some peace and quiet, so she will allow no visitors apart from the small bird that sits patiently on a branch outside his window and sings all day long with a strange quiver to its voice. Her husband does not appear to mind, but he has no strength to say much about anything these days. He is far too weak to read the newspaper or to take an interest in the world about him, but behind his closed eyes, and in his tired mind, he clearly sees the black sail slowly approaching across the bright water. Sunrise brings no respite, and each day the doctor visits twice, once in the morning and again in the evening, and Mother leaves this man alone in the bedroom with Mr. Williams. When the doctor emerges the man's deportment seldom changes for, while he has no desire to alarm Mrs. Williams, he also has no intention of misleading her. The doctor always gathers his belongings and bids her farewell having said as little as possible to Mrs. Williams beyond confirming that the pneumonia still has her husband in its grip.

My husband asks without having to spend any words. With his eyes only he makes it clear to me what he desires and I cannot refuse him. First, I approach and help him to sit upright in the bed. The doctor insists that the fresh white sheets be changed every other day, but each evening, before he sleeps, I change the sheets and then I help him into a clean set of pajamas. I look forward to this intimate part of our day when I am able to do for him what nobody else can. I often find I have to deftly shave the portions of his face where I have forgotten to apply the blade, or take a damp handkerchief and clean the sleep from his eyes or the cold from his classic nose. On this bright March morning, as impatient spring tries once more to move with a quick, short stride and leave winter behind, I help my husband to sit upright for without resorting to any words he has made it clear what he desires. When I am sure that his back is properly supported with pillows, only then do I open the bottom drawer of the bureau. I offer him the mirror, which he holds by the handle, and I watch as he is shaken into panic by the puzzled face in the glass. He eventually absorbs the initial distress of recognition, and I stand patiently to one side, but I know that once the mirror is in his hands my husband is no longer with me. I know that my husband will spend the whole day staring into the mirror, at first tormenting himself, and then comforting his spirit with happier memories, but his well-disciplined countenance will betray little of this inner drama. I watch him carefully and listen closely for in the distance I can hear mortality, like dull thunder, continuing to rumble its merciless way toward him and I take this quaking as a signal that I should withdraw for my husband's daily performances with the handheld mirror require no audience.

My sleeping wife lies next to me. When she opens her eyes she will discover that I have already left and entered the darkness where I search now for my father. As I look all around I realize that I can see nothing. In fact, I can no longer even see myself, but I truly lost sight of myself many years ago when my tightly shod young feet touched the shore of the powerful country to the north. I followed my father, for he said that it would be all right, and I continued to follow him, but I lost him on that New York night when, freshly arrived from the west coast, he sat upstairs in nigger heaven and looked down on me. Father! I shout now in the darkness, but I hear only the echo of my own voice. Father! The truth is, once he left nigger heaven he never seemed to find a way back to me, or to himself. Father, are you there? Father? And now I am alone in the darkness and beyond my wife, who sleeps peacefully, unaware of the fact that she has been abandoned. Father, do you *really* understand what they want from us in this American world? Do you? We are being held hostage as performers, and those who imagine that they are engaged in something other than entertainment should ask my wife to pass them the handheld mirror. But I must not complain for my time has been spent, and I have no more time, and I wander in this darkness that makes human beings of us all. *(Father! Where are you?)* Here in the darkness, beyond my wife, my journey is over and I shall perform no more. I will no longer be tormented with the anxiety of being the sole representative in the room. Never again will I be the only one onstage, wondering what they see when they look at me. I will never again be frightened to look too closely at myself. Blackbird. It is unfair to ask a man to travel his one precious life bearing this burden, and I am tired, so please leave me alone in the darkness and let me search for my father, who is also lost. Others will come after me to entertain you, and they will happily change their name and put on whatever clownish costume you wish them to wear, and dance, and sing, and perform in a manner that will amuse you, and you *will* mimic them, and you *will* make your money, but know that at the darkest point of the night, when no eyes are upon them, these people's souls will be heavy, and eventually some among them will say no, and you will see their sadness, and then you will turn from them and choose somebody else to place in the empty room, or nudge onto your empty stage, but it will not be me for I am tired, so please excuse me and let me wander here in the darkness and search for my father, who is also lost. That is all I ask, that you please just let me be.

Epilogue

Epilogue

Scores of umbrellas raise their heads to greet the torrential rain. On this icy day the cold wind funnels down broad Harlem avenues, but this has not deterred fifteen thousand mourners from standing in silent tribute outside of St. Philip's Church to acknowledge a forty-seven-year-old man who was, in his day, the most famous colored man in America. Mrs. Lottie Williams follows the bearers out of the church, and the crowd can now see that she has chosen to wear a somber hat and veil to match her elegant black gown. In her heart Lottie wishes that on this day she were able to stand before her husband bareheaded. She wishes to give everything, the whole truth, to her husband, but decorum demands otherwise. Lottie looks on as the men carefully transfer the metallic casket, which is covered with white roses, and orchids, and lilies, into the waiting hearse, and as they do so she remembers the tall, elegant young man that she met in a photographer's studio who seemed to possess grace and breeding that came from another world. As she shields her eyes from the driving rain, it comforts her to think that even as she looks on, her dear Bert is probably making his slow way back to the peace of his lost world.

He has heard that anything is possible in the big country to the north. His father has told him this, and he understands that this is the reason why they are leaving their beaches, and abandoning their island. His father is giving them both a chance to improve themselves in the land of opportunity to the north, but freedom comes with a price. He knows this now, but back then, as they stood together after a sudden downpour and watched ribbons of water fall from the palm fronds and groove trenches into their earth, he omitted to mention this fact. Back then, father and son stood together on the beach and waited patiently to welcome back the running tide, their dreams working in tandem, but now the son has paid the price and his journey is concluded. Somewhere in the darkness he will discover his father, and then he will discover George, who will once more be by his side, and together the two men will look back as far as the Barbary Coast and the corner of Market Street where two real coons determined that they would do something more than buck-dance and grin for America, and then, when George needs to rest, Bert alone can look back to the Bahamas of his birth, where a tall gangly eleven-year-old boy let the sand ease its way between his toes as he stood idly on a beach and wondered what would become of him in the country to the north that his beloved father seemed so determined to embrace.